Simplicity

A Simple Love Story: Book 1

Dana LeCheminant

First Printing: October 2019

ISBN: 978-1-951753-00-9

To my sister and my college ladies:
this book never would have seen the light of day
without its first fans

CHAPTER ONE

"Perfection is essential." My mother's mantra always popped into my head at the worst moments, like when I was just about to put the finishing touches on the painting I'd been working on all morning. I blamed the fact she'd gone on a bit of a tirade at breakfast that ended with, "If you're not perfect, Lanna, you're coming up short." That sentence alone had convinced me to get out of the house and blast some music through my headphones to drown her words out.

Most of the time I ignored her little comments, since I had very little chance of ever coming close to her idea of perfection, but this time I was finding it difficult to get her out of my head, as if she were looking over my shoulder at the easel in front of me. Usually the music worked and distracted me well enough, but I'd given up on that hours ago so I could just focus on what I was doing.

I'd been painting for years, and most days I could accept when something was finished and move on. This particular canvas, however, kept giving me trouble, and I was running out of patience trying to fix something that didn't look broken. The mountainscape was beautiful, really, probably one of the best scenes I'd painted yet, though nothing close to what real artists could produce. But there was something missing. Maybe another tree?

I leaned back a little to get a more distant look, noticing for the first time that rain pounded on the roof of the stables where I'd hidden myself to avoid my mother's constant criticisms of how I was "coming up short." She'd been especially bad today and seemed convinced I would either end up alone or a lesbian if I didn't snag myself a husband soon. I suspected that was because Chandler Wixcomb was back in town, and he was one of the few eligible bachelors I hadn't blown my chances with yet. Honestly, I couldn't see why he would still be interested, especially because we didn't even use our stables for horses, which were Chandler's passion. If he knew the only things in this massive building were a bunch of dusty saddles and for some reason a broken down motorcycle, Chandler would probably write me off like the rest of the rich folk and go fall in love with a horse instead of a human, since I was pretty sure the animals were the only thing that came up to snuff for the guy.

I certainly didn't meet his expectations, though that hadn't stopped him from texting me a couple hours ago to tell me about his new thoroughbred. Apparently she was magnificent, but I hadn't bothered sending a response. Chandler Wixcomb didn't want me, anyway, and he would figure that out soon enough.

As Mother often said, though I was passable, I wasn't the prettiest or the smartest, and what little I had to offer probably came from the fortune I would inherit from my parents when they kicked the bucket. At twenty-five, apparently I'd wasted my best years and the only thing I had left of value wasn't even mine yet, which was why she worked so hard to make me presentable to the men in our social circle.

Dear mother was convinced a woman had no chance in life without a man to take care of her. I was pretty sure she was meant to have been born in the nineteenth century instead of the twenty-first.

I squinted at my painting in the low light as the rain thundered a little harder overhead. Maybe if I added a few more clouds…

"This is really good."

I shrieked at the sound of a strange voice above me, leaping sideways and slipping on a stray piece of hay. I went flying backward into my easel and crashing on the floor in a painful heap, and I had to untangle my legs from my stool before I managed to get my hands underneath me and sit up, ready to try to defend myself.

A young man stood in the stall next to mine, his arms resting on the wall between us as he belted out laughter that filled the whole stables. I'd never seen him before in my life, and my already racing heart skipped into overtime. I was under attack!

"Who are you?" I tried to ask, but it came out as a gasp.

"Sorry," he replied, still laughing. "I didn't mean to scare you."

I couldn't breathe. My paint pallet stuck to my shoulder, and my ankle throbbed from twisting when I fell, and I could feel a good many bruises popping up. But I ignored all of that because I couldn't get enough air to focus on anything, especially not on the stranger who stepped around the stall and crouched next to me.

"You okay there?" I thought he asked and reached out his hand to peel the pallet from my sleeve. At least he looked concerned now instead of amused.

I swallowed, and with immense effort I took a deep breath. Suddenly I was less dizzy and more aware, and my eyes locked on his. And then I froze, staring at him like my body no longer knew how to function, all motor skills gone. Maybe he wasn't there to attack me, or he would have done so already, but that didn't make him any less anxiety-inducing when he watched me so intently.

His smile returned, which didn't help the pounding in my chest. Goodness, that was quite the smile. "There you go," he said gently. "Generally, breathing is a good thing."

"Who are you?" I said again, this time able to actually say real words now that I had some air in my lungs. "Why are you…"

"Sneaking around empty stables?" he finished for me. Holding out his hand, he helped me to my feet and took a step back, which made me feel at least a little more comfortable, though I wasn't much enjoying how he stood in my only path of escape. "I was told I could find the lawn mower in here."

"The lawn…" He was a new gardener? Oh. But we had plenty of those. I tried to stay focused. "No," I said. "No, I think they keep those in the shed." I was staring at him and I knew it, but I couldn't stop. Being paraded around the rich and elite by my mother, I had seen my fair share of handsome men, but this guy had a different appeal to him. Tanned and muscular, he obviously spent a lot of time outside—of course he did, if he was a gardener—and he was probably stronger than anyone I knew, even if he wasn't very tall. Based on those shoulders alone… His dark hair fell onto his forehead, and I could only imagine the life it had when it wasn't stuck to his skin with rain. But his eyes. Good glory, his eyes. I'd never seen eyes so dark, but they were the warmest things I'd ever seen. I knew if I wasn't careful I could get lost in those eyes.

"The shed," he repeated, and his half grin made me slightly dizzy again. "That would make more sense. I'm starting to think Javier is just messing with me now, because it's not like I can mow the lawn today anyway." He gestured toward the ceiling, where the rain still pattered, but then his eyes slid to my overturned canvas.

"Sorry," he said again. "I really didn't mean to laugh, but I have never seen anyone jump as high as you just did. If I had known you would react like that, I would have coughed or something before I spoke. Did you really paint that?"

Folding my arms, I tried not to take that as an insult. Luckily, I had had a lot of practice learning how to let criticism bounce off me. *Thanks, Mother.* "Are you really surprised?" I asked, trying—and probably failing—to sound as haughty as my mother. Who was this guy who thought he could just waltz into my haven and tell me there was no way I could have done something at least moderately skilled?

He fought back a grin and rolled his eyes at me. Apparently he had failed to learn that rolling your eyes was unacceptable, something my mother told me often. "That's not what I meant," he said then picked up my canvas, examining it as he brushed off a couple pieces of straw. Like he would have any idea what good art looked like. "I just never knew the Davenport Princess had a talent like this."

My eyes went wide. "What did you just call me?"

His gaze strayed from the painting and swept over me, but only for a moment. "You heard me," he said as he cocked his head. "Where is this, anyway?"

Davenport Princess? Did people really call me that, or was he just trying to get under my skin? I didn't like either option, and neither did I like the fact that he kept frowning as his eyes followed the lines of my brush. "It's no-where," I said, the words coming out stilted. "Don't you have somewhere to be?" As much as I had to admit I liked looking at him, his unwavering exam-ination was making me uncomfortable. I would almost rather face my mother's all-seeing eye than have my art under scrutiny like this. My paintings were the only form of expression I had, and there was a reason I kept them to myself.

Throwing me another glance, he bent down and picked up the easel so he could return the canvas to where it belonged. Luckily, the painting had been mostly dry when I collided with it and looked pretty undamaged. Without answering my question, the guy looked at me and asked, "Have you ever tried painting somewhere real?"

I thought his eyes on my painting were bad. It was even worse when he was looking right at me, as if those dark eyes were looking right into my soul. I took it back. I would rather he looked at my painting instead of making me feel exposed like this. Besides, his question was so far from what I expected that I wasn't sure how to answer it. "Why would I do that?" I asked. "That's no fun."

His half grin was back, making my face burn because he refused to even blink as he watched me. "You haven't been anywhere, have you?"

"Of course I…" But I couldn't finish. Despite my family's money, I'd never even left the city, and I had no plans to anytime soon. I was perfectly content to keep my feet on the ground where they belonged. "What does it matter?" I amended. "I like using my imagination."

"And your imagination is great," he assured me. "But it lacks heart. It just has no…" He waved a hand around the painting. "Soul."

Excuse me?

"Oh, don't look at me like that. I'm not saying it's bad. You still have some awesome talent."

I'd had enough. "I'm pretty sure Javi will be wondering where you are," I said sharply as I began gathering up my supplies from where they'd been scattered. "And you clearly don't know what you're talking about."

He simply laughed and backed out of the stable, his eyes still on me. "Don't I?" he said just before reaching the doors. And then he was gone, disappearing into the heavy rain.

What was that all about? I realized too late that he'd never told me his name, and though he mentioned Javier, I wasn't completely convinced he worked for our head gardener at all. And who did he think he was, going around scaring people and telling them they didn't know how to paint with their heart? As if he had any idea what—

"Ah crap," I said out loud as my eyes again landed on the painting I'd spent hours on. I didn't know how I hadn't picked up on that as the problem, but he was completely right. It was just a couple of pointy purple mountains. Some lifeless trees. Even the sky looked dull and empty, though I'd spent a good half hour on the clouds alone. How did I not realize how juvenile the whole thing looked? I wasn't even sure if I could do anything to fix it because it was so bad.

And suddenly I was afraid to go back and look at my other works. Either I was having an off day, or I didn't know as much about art as I'd thought.

Neither option gave me much comfort.

* * *

"Oh Lanna," my mother sighed as soon as I stepped inside the house.

In my defense, I'd done everything in my power to avoid tracking mud across the floor, since I knew our maid worked hard to keep things spotless enough for my mother. I'd tried to avoid the gravel path that led from the house to the stables, keeping mainly to the grass, and I even left my shoes outside and squeezed rain from my hair before coming in. But I couldn't do anything about the state of my clothes.

"Did you roll around in the dirt?" Mother asked in exasperation. "And how on earth did you manage to get so much paint on yourself?"

I glanced at my shoulder, where my sleeve was smeared with blue, red, and yellow paint. I'd done worse, I decided, and it only added a little more personality to my paint shirt.

But then my mother shrieked, making me jump, and I quickly looked down at my feet to make sure her pristine tile wasn't muddied. She, however, grabbed a handful of hair and held it out as if I'd done something horrendous.

"It's just a little paint," I mumbled, knowing it wouldn't make a difference. She *treasured* my hair, since I was the only one of her three children to have inherited her blonde. Both my brothers had ended up brunette.

"Can't you switch to watercolors?" she moaned, and I almost thought she was on the verge of tears.

What would she do, I wondered, *if I showed up one day with a black pixie cut?* I didn't know if I would have the courage to do something like that, but I did enjoy imagining her minor stroke. "Watercolors have no room for error," I replied, using the same argument I used every time she tried to convince me to go with a medium slightly less damaging than acrylic or oil. "I just need to wash it out, so stop freaking out."

Pouting—grown women really shouldn't pout—she put her fingers to her temples and shut her eyes. "We barely have time for that."

I didn't like the sound of that. "Uh, why?"

She looked at me as if I should already know, which I didn't. "Your father has a new client," she said simply.

My father was a highly skilled and sought-after corporate lawyer. He had new clients all the time. If she was telling me about it, it had to mean the news had something to do with me. "So?" I asked, wishing I hadn't.

Sighing, she put her hand on my arm and gave me a look that clearly said she had very little faith in me anymore. "This client is Gilroy Munroe."

"Isn't there some sort of client confidentiality agreement you're break-ing?" I replied, but I couldn't help but be intrigued. Gilroy Munroe was the largest art dealer on the West Coast, and he was known for acquiring incred-ibly rare works. I'd been dying to see his latest gallery collection before it went to auction, but it was clear on the other side of the city. Getting there had been a problem.

Brushing off my question, my mother put on a fake smile and continued, "Your father is meeting with Munroe this evening, and he has invited us along."

Either my father suddenly possessed uncharacteristic sympathy toward my hobbies, or my mother had weaseled her way into the invitation, which filled me with dread. The only reason she would bring me along and risk me embarrassing her would be because there was someone else who would be at this meeting.

"Who is he?" I grumbled. "The man you want me to meet. Not Gilroy Munroe?"

Her laugh was sharp and cold. "Don't be ridiculous. You could never be on the same level as someone like Gilroy. He's in a league of his own."

"Then who?" I pressed.

"Obviously his son," she replied. "Aaron, I think it was. I hear he's very handsome."

"And probably as pigheaded as the rest," I mumbled under my breath. Most likely worse. Gilroy Munroe was the king of high-end art, a well-known millionaire who probably sat in his vault every night counting his gold. Any child that came from that could only be just as vain and greedy. A prince in every sense of the word.

"Oh don't make that face," my mother scoffed and shoved me toward the stairs so I could start getting the paint out of my hair. "One of these days, Lanna, you'll eventually figure out that your choices are dwindling. This could be your last hope, and I'm not about to give up on you."

After reaching my room, I paused in front of my most favorite painting I'd ever done. It was nothing special, just a single sunflower, but it was the first thing I ever did that made me feel like I was actually good at something. It was the only reason Mother even allowed me to paint as often as I did, since it had won me a couple awards in high school.

Looking at it now, I felt a coldness settle inside me that had nothing to do with the rain soaked into my clothes. The new gardener was right. Though I'd captured the essence of a sunflower and gotten every detail just right from my imagination, it had no life to it. It was lacking the simplicity of mimicking something real, and that bothered me more than it should. Sure, I was young when I painted it, but, looking around, I was pretty sure I hadn't improved much in the ten years since.

I had to make myself somewhat presentable for my meeting with the 'Prince of Art,' and yet all I wanted to do was paint something to prove that gardener wrong, to show him that I could put heart into a painting, that I wasn't just a princess doomed to live out my perfect, soulless life in luxury.

CHAPTER TWO

As I found out seconds before stepping through the door, "meeting your father's client" was code for attending one of the largest fundraising galas of the year. I should have suspected when my mother insisted I wear a floor length, dark blue evening gown that there was something more at play, but I'd gotten so used to her antics that it didn't even cross my mind until we walked up to the venue and I caught sight of the banners bearing photos of starving children in Central America.

"Why?" I asked simply as we joined the short line leading inside.

With her perfect smile firmly in place, my mother tucked her arm through mine. Probably to make sure I didn't run, though I wasn't sure I could have in the heels she made me wear. "It's for the children," she said.

"Haven't the children suffered enough?" I moaned. I shifted my weight from foot to foot, trying to ease the pain of walking in heels for an extended period of time. I had tried to sneak out in flats, but I hadn't even gotten to the bottom of the stairs before she caught me.

"You know," she said, leaning close, "you wouldn't have so many problems if you didn't insist on walking everywhere."

I didn't reply to that one, and my mother didn't push the issue. In that regard, at least, I could count on her to keep her mouth shut. She knew my reasons for avoiding cars.

"And I didn't trick you," she added.

Confused, I stared at her as Father reached into his tux jacket for our invitation. "I never said you did," I replied.

"You were thinking it. I know that look."

Maybe she wasn't as clueless as I thought, but I decided to play dumb. "What do you mean?"

"Your father really is here to meet with Munroe. It's his charity event, after all."

"Oh." I glanced at the banner again as we walked inside, noticing for the first time Gilroy Munroe's name at the bottom. My cheeks blossomed with heat, and for a moment I felt a little bad.

But only until she opened her mouth again: "Oh Lanna, you still have paint in your hair. Why did I have to get cursed with you as a daughter? Your cousin Catherine isn't like this."

That was because my cousin Catherine was spoiled rotten and constantly getting into trouble. I hadn't even seen her since she was five or six, but the stories of her East coast teenage escapades had made their way to our side of the country and left me shocked. I didn't want to be anything like her.

"Love you too," I grumbled as Mother detached herself from me to go greet her gaggle of trophy wives who had set up shop in the center of the massive, glittering room. My father had already wandered off, leaving me standing alone at the side of the gala and hoping one of the wait staff would come this way with champagne. I wasn't much prone to drinking, but it certainly helped make evenings like this more bearable. Mother would return as soon as she'd offered devastating comments to her "friends," and then I would have to endure her matchmaking antics for the rest of the evening.

Until I could get a flute of alcohol in my hand, I took to people watching. And there were many of them.

Most of the attendees I already knew. There were only so many people in my parents' social circle, since millionaires could be hard to come by, and I'd gotten used to seeing the same faces no matter where we went. Victoria Donovan was in the dead center of the room as always, a new beau on her arm even as she flirted with the Connelly brothers. Mrs. Morales's laughter echoed across the crowded room as her husband probably told yet another Alaskan fishing story to those around them. Chase Thicke was already drunk and dancing to the music, even though the string quartet played gentle classical in the background.

One man I didn't recognize stood near the far corner, four different ladies vying for his attention. He was handsome, sure, as the wealthy could often be, but I couldn't figure out why Sarah Huxton and Geneva Kennedy would be giving each other death glares over him, especially because he hardly seemed to pay attention to any of the girls who surrounded him. He kept his head high and his square jaw tight, and he looked over the heads of his admirers with a look of disdain, almost disgust.

A man had to be really high and mighty to ignore someone like Geneva Kennedy so easily, and I immediately disliked him.

"Lanna!" My mother's voice carried across the room easily, though I still debated if I could get away with ignoring her. But she was quickly at my side, her claws on my shoulder. "There he is," she said, pointing. "Your future."

I followed her finger to any number of guys, most of whom I'd already rejected. "Which one?" I asked, nerves churning in my stomach. There was no way. It couldn't possibly be him.

"That one," she said, way too loud. How had she found champagne already? "The tall one in the corner that the Kennedy girl is drooling over."

Of course it was. That was what I got for hoping there could be at least one decent man among the elite. Apparently I was doomed to be thrown at all the smug, snobby rich boys until my mother gave up or I got too old to be appealing anymore.

"Let's go introduce you."

The blood drained from my face. "What? No!" Especially not with all those far superior women standing there.

But my mother wrapped her impossibly strong fingers around my wrist and started dragging me through the milling crowd, ignoring the annoyed looks we got from those she pushed past as if we were much more important. Was that why the gardener called me a princess? How would he even know?

"Mr. Munroe!" my mother said sweetly as soon as we were in earshot. The other ladies had impressive glares, and my face burned the second 'The Prince' looked our way, his eyes cold. I didn't care if his father had built an empire around art, not if he would always look at me like that.

"Mrs. Davenport," he said after he'd taken us in.

My mother giggled, and in that moment I vowed to never laugh anything like her. Not if it would make me sound that ridiculous. "You know who I am?" she asked, as if nothing in the world could make her happier.

The young Munroe shook his head, and then suddenly he untangled himself from his horde of admirers and led us a few feet away. Surprising. "Only through others," he corrected, "but I've heard a lot about you. And you," he added, turning his gaze to me.

Up close, his eyes were so much softer than I expected, and for a moment their deep blue made me forget how to function. How he managed to give me such a searching look without making me feel exposed and found wanting, I had no idea, and I stared at him as I tried to understand what could possibly make him different from the rest of the room. A jab from my mother knocked sense back into me, and I extended my hand. "Lanna," I said, my face burning even brighter.

He smiled briefly. "Adam," he returned, his hand warm and soft around mine.

"Why don't I let you two talk," my mother said, giving me a not so subtle wink then disappearing.

I realized my hand was still in Adam's, and I pulled it free. "I'm sorry," I said, barely more than a mumble.

"About what?" he replied.

I nodded toward my mother's retreating frame. "That. She's…" How best to word it? "Crazy."

Adam chuckled, and I felt a strange sense of pride for being able to make him laugh. I didn't do that often. With anyone. They usually just gave me weird looks and found an excuse to leave. "She's a mother," he said with a shrug. "They're all a little crazy."

Geneva Kennedy was glaring at me so hard I was waiting for my hair to catch fire. Turning so she was out of my sightline, I tried to remember how to act like a normal human. Generally I didn't care what these men thought of me, but for some reason, I didn't want this one to think I was completely pathetic. If I was going to be stuck talking to him—I could feel my mother's eyes on me from the other side of the room—I was going to try to enjoy the evening.

"This is a really great charity," I tried. "And your father really brought out a good crowd for a good cause."

Adam's eyes traveled the guests. "Yes," he said, and there was an undercurrent of irritation in his voice. "My father. Quite the philanthropist."

I wasn't sure how to respond to the bitterness I heard. Was he trying to say his father didn't care about hungry Colombian kids? If that was the case, he didn't need to stress about it. No one in the room cared. They just came to look good and throw their money around.

"Sorry," he said before I could find something to say. "I shouldn't…"

I guessed he wasn't going to finish that sentence. "Do you come to these events often?" I asked. "I don't know if I've seen you before." And I was pretty sure I would have remembered him, given his strong features. Sarah Huxton certainly didn't go for the plain ones.

He clenched his jaw, the muscles tight. "No," he said after a moment. "I've tried to avoid these things when I can."

I was immediately jealous that he had managed to do it for so long. My mother always had a solution for every excuse I gave. "So what changed?" I asked. Maybe I could learn something from this Prince of Art who had managed to stay off the marriage market.

Adam sighed, folding his arms. "I'm getting more into the business, so my dad decided I needed to make a public appearance for once."

"You know art too?" I blurted out.

Obviously hearing the eagerness in my voice, Adam cocked his head at me. Behind him, Geneva Kennedy slowly circled closer, though I didn't think he noticed. "I take it you're an art fan," he said.

I tried not to be too disappointed that he didn't answer the question, which probably meant he only handled the business side of things and not the acquisitions. "Sort of," I replied, making sure I sounded calm. Normal. All the while an amused voice spoke in the back of my head telling me I didn't know art like I thought because I didn't know how to capture heart. *Stupid gardener.*

Adam's eyes suddenly locked on something behind me, and he nodded his head once. "Excuse me," he said before stepping past me and into the crowd.

Great.

Geneva and Sarah were both right behind him, and Geneva gave me a sneer as she passed. "Better luck next time, Princess," she said and slinked off after Adam. So they did call me that. *Awesome.*

Before I knew it, my mother was back at my side and beaming like I'd just won Miss America. "That was excellent," she said, brushing a stray strand of hair behind my ear. "You'll have The Prince of Art in love with you in no time."

I only sighed in reply. Not that I cared, but I was pretty sure the so-called prince had plenty of better options, and our short conversation was the only one we would ever have. It was better that way, and no amount of scheming could make something happen if Adam had no interest, which he clearly didn't. Not that I wanted anything to happen, of course.

But that wasn't about to stop my mother, and I could see the gleam in her eyes. I knew this was far from over.

"Just tell me when we can go home," I muttered and grabbed the nearest flute of champagne.

CHAPTER THREE

The Saturday sun beckoned me outside just after breakfast, and before I could chicken out, I grabbed my supplies and hiked across the flat lawns to the natural pond out back by the tree line that bordered the property wall. It wasn't all that large of a pond and could have been four times its size without cutting into the sheer size of our backyard much more than it already did, but it was still one of my favorite places on the estate. There was something wild about it. Imperfect. And it was far enough away from the house that my mother couldn't see me through any of the windows, which by itself made it an ideal place to paint. I wouldn't even be bothered by the many landscapers who spent their days keeping the massive grounds pristine, though I could hear a leaf blower off in the distance.

I needed this time to be alone and concentrate. I could paint something real. I knew I could, and I told myself that this was only to prove to myself and get rid of my doubts. It had nothing to do with the gardener from the stables.

I sat on my favorite bench next to the water, stretched out my fingers, then went to work.

Many hours later, I was pretty sure I'd managed to capture the pond fairly well. Even the ripples in the water where the tiny stream came in glittered with sunlight, and while I still had a lot of work to do on the grasses and daffodils within the rocks around the pond, the painting was coming along nicely. I just needed to touch up a part of the—

"Not bad," the gardener said behind me.

My hand slipped, my brush striping a streak of gray through the middle of my pond. "Are you kidding me?" I growled and stood to get angry.

He was literally right behind me, and I was so caught off guard by his closeness that my foot slipped. If he hadn't grabbed my hand, I would have ended up in the pond, soaking wet and furious.

He laughed, and the sound sent my nerves skittering even more. "I'm so sorry," he said, though I wasn't sure he meant it. "That's surprisingly fun to do."

Tearing my hand free, I glared at him then settled back on the bench before I really fell over. "I could get you fired, you know."

"Yeah," he agreed. "You could. I see you took my advice." Nodding to my painting, he sat next to me.

I scooted to the opposite end of the bench. I really wished I could tell him he was full of himself, but he'd probably see right through that. So I settled with, "Maybe."

His eyes were still really dark, but out in the sunlight they had a little more gold to them. And they were locked on my canvas, taking it all in. "I mean, it's better," he started.

Seriously? It was probably my best recreation ever. I folded my arms, somehow knowing he had more to say.

"But you've probably sat by this pond for years, haven't you?" he asked.

"So?"

"So you're probably painting how you think it should feel. Not how it actually does."

I stared at him, failing to come up with a reason why he was so determined to make me feel completely untalented. Either my few art classes were a waste of money, or he was spewing complete crap just to torment me. I didn't like either option.

"Well how would you paint it then?" I asked, my frustration clear in my voice. I tossed my brush at him, which he caught easily before it splattered paint on his dirt-streaked shirt.

"Oh I don't paint," he replied and spun the brush in his fingers. "Though I've always wanted to learn. Maybe you could teach me."

I tensed as the sun beat down, suddenly hot and unbearable. "You're insane," I decided out loud. "And you have no idea what you're talking about." Without even bothering to grab my things, I hopped up and started heading back to the house.

"Wait!" he called, though the word got lost in his laughter. He caught up to me and blocked my path, his smile apologetic. "I'm sorry. What I wanted to say was you should try painting something you've never seen before. It'll help keep your mind out of the work so you can use your heart instead. It's good practice, until you can figure it out."

It wasn't an awful idea, but that didn't mean I had any intention of doing it. "Yeah," I grumbled sarcastically, "I'll just go somewhere random. Because that's possible."

His smile morphed into one of confusion. "Isn't it? You have a car, don't you?"

Why couldn't I have just kept walking away? "Well yeah," I replied.

"Doesn't mean I know how to drive it."

His eyes went wide, and heat rose on my cheeks until I was pretty sure I was bright red. "Wait," he said. "You don't know how to drive? You're how old?"

"That's not important," I replied through my teeth.

"Did your parents not teach you? They didn't even send you to that fancy driving school all you rich folk use?"

I didn't want to have this conversation. In fact, I wasn't keen on *any* conversation with this guy who seemed to spend more time scaring me than he did doing his job. "I have somewhere to be," I said, and my voice got lost in my throat. Was I crying? Seriously? It was time to head inside before I further embarrassed myself.

I tried to step around him, but the stupid gardener grabbed my shoulder and looked so sympathetic that I couldn't help but want to let him keep talking, if only to hear what he had to say before I walked away.

"I didn't mean to offend you," he said carefully. "Lots of people don't know how to drive. I didn't even get my license until I was eighteen." I sensed more to that story when his ears pinked a little. "Anyway, if you want, I can take you somewhere to paint. I know the perfect place."

The perfect place to kill me, probably. "I don't even know you," I argued, only afterward realizing that I should have used a stronger argument when he brought back his breathtaking smile.

"Oh. Where are my manners?"

"Took the words right out of my mouth," I replied dryly.

He just laughed and held out his hand. "Luke Hawthorne," he said. "If it helps, I had to pass a background check before I came to work here, and I have one of those fancy little badges to let me in and out of the front gate." He pulled it from his pocket to show me. "I'm twenty-eight, a Cancer, and I like long walks on the beach."

I fought the smile playing at my lips, which became even harder when he realized he was breaking me and widened his own grin.

"Haven't you ever wanted to see something outside these walls?" he asked, his voice so suddenly soft that I had to lean closer to hear him. "Outside the city?"

"Don't you have work to do?" I asked lamely.

He didn't move. "That can wait," he said. "You can't."

He still held his hand out for me to shake, and I knew that if I took that hand, I would be doing something I had never had the courage to do. Leave the city? Go off on some adventure without my parents half a step behind me? Two days ago I would have laughed at the idea. But last night I had met likely the last option for any kind of "appropriate" future according to my mother, and there was nothing about me that appealed to him. I had blown all my chances, and my life would probably be chosen for me. Did I really have anything left to lose?

Luke held his hand just a little closer, his eyes dancing as he watched my resolve slip. "Live a little, Princess," he said.

I didn't know what had changed in me, but suddenly I found myself reaching out and grasping his fingers.

* * *

I'd never been so tense. I barely managed to put on my seatbelt in Luke's worn out truck before he shot out onto the street, and I had to grab onto the handle next to me to keep my hands from shaking. I could do this. I would be fine. I could do it.

It only took two minutes before Luke glanced over at me and realized my knuckles were white. "You aren't going to get in trouble, are you?" he asked, worry in his voice that barely carried over the rock music blaring from the radio. All the sounds around me blurred into a mess of noise that made me dizzy.

I shook my head, but I was afraid that if I opened my mouth I would throw up. I probably *would* get in trouble, but I could handle that.

"I'm not going to hurt you," he said, trying again to guess the reason for the anxiety that glued me to the back of my seat.

"I know," I whispered quickly and closed my eyes. Nope. That was worse.

I felt the truck slow a little and looked over at him in surprise. He kept glancing away from the road and at me, understanding brightening his eyes. "You're afraid," he realized. "That's why you don't drive." There wasn't any mocking in his words. Just sympathy. "I've never been in an accident," he assured me, "and I've been driving for fifteen years. You'll be fine."

"It's not you I'm worried about," I replied. There were so many cars on the road. So many people to watch out for. He couldn't control everything.

Luke reached out and spun the volume down until the music was just a soft noise in the background. "What happened?" he asked gently.

I waited until he pulled off the main road and into a neighborhood, where fewer cars joined us on the road. I could breathe a little easier there. "My brother," I said. I swallowed then kept going. "Ben. When I was fourteen, he was working as a driver for someone. I don't even know who."

A couple cars passed us quickly, and I sucked in my breath sharply, holding it until they were gone. Luke just kept driving, and though he was silent and kept his eyes on the road, I somehow knew he was listening to every word. I had no idea why I was telling him all of this, but that didn't stop me from saying it.

"He was driving his boss after a party or something late one night," I said, trying not to choke on my words. It wasn't like I had never told anyone the story, but this time felt different. "There was a drunk driver," I continued. "Ben saw her coming, and he turned the car so…so the other driver hit the front of his car, instead of the back, where his boss sat. Ben was dead on impact."

I brushed a tear from my cheek and took a deep breath to stop myself from breaking into sobs like I tended to do when it came to my oldest brother. Losing Ben had been bad enough, but it felt like I'd lost my other brother Matthew at the same time. After that funeral, Matthew had lost his light, and I'd barely seen him since. One tiny moment on a San Francisco street, and I'd lost the only family I cared about. "Sorry," I mumbled. "I know men hate crying."

Luke made a sound, though I wasn't sure if it was a scoff or a laugh. "Who told you that?" he asked. "Because I cry all the time."

I scowled at him. "No you don't."

"Yes I do," he argued. "Movies, weddings, those little animal shelter commercials. I fall apart."

I laughed, and suddenly my body relaxed a little. I could breathe again, and Luke watched me out of the corner of his eye with his little half grin warming the space between us.

"I'm sorry about your brother," he said. "Losing people you care about is never easy. Especially when they're young like that."

I had so many questions. His expression told me there was so much more to his comment, and I was pretty sure he had lost someone too, but I didn't have the courage to ask him. I was used to my own sadness, but I wasn't sure if I could handle someone else's.

So instead I looked out the window and changed the subject: "Where are we going, anyway?"

The neighborhood had started to thin, the houses bigger and farther between. It looked a lot like my own neighborhood, but without the pretentiousness that came with it. The yards were a little less cared for, the houses themselves older and more weathered. The road kept winding higher up a hill, and Luke kept pushing his truck onward with no indication of stopping.

"I told you," he replied, a bit of mischief in his voice. "Somewhere special. It'll inspire you."

"If you think a few trees and some grassy hills are inspiring," I argued.

He laughed, and I found myself grinning back at him. "Just wait," he said and kept driving.

I watched the road change from two lanes to one. The houses disappeared, as did the fences and any kind of grooming. The landscape grew wilder, wildflowers blooming along the road and trees growing low and gnarled instead of tall and symmetrical. Birds flitted through the trees, and at one point I could have sworn I saw the flash of a red fox tail disappear into the grass.

I wasn't sure how long we'd been driving when Luke pulled the truck to a stop outside an old building. Boards covered the windows, and vines did their best to overpower the domed roof, but the thing stood strong if not loved. I vaguely remembered going there with my class as a kid, but it had been years.

I followed Luke out of the truck and looked up at the large building. It had a lot of character, definitely, but it wouldn't make a very interesting painting. "You want me to paint the observatory?" I asked.

Grabbing my stuff from the back of the truck, Luke grinned. "Nah. Though I'm sure it would look great."

"What then?"

"This way," he replied and headed around the side of the building with my paints in tow.

I followed warily. I'd already decided I could mostly trust the gardener (though that was probably a horrible decision, really), but we were a long ways away from anyone else if something went wrong. A quick check of my phone told me I didn't even have cell service up here, and I couldn't decide if the swirling in my stomach was from uneasiness or excitement. Probably a little bit of both. I had never done anything like this. My mother literally knew where I was every second of every day, and if she knew I'd run off with the gardener…

I laughed a little to myself at the thought. The horror stories she would come up with if she ever found out would be endless. *Who will take you now?* she would moan. *Now you're going to end up homeless with half a dozen little brats hanging on you night and day and no way to feed them!* I half wondered if she would convince my father to disown me if I chose a path that wasn't hers. It had happened to my brother Matthew, and I was smart enough to know my mother kept that threat hanging over my head as leverage, whether or not she said the words out loud.

Luke suddenly appeared at my side, scaring me out of my wits. Luckily, though my heart skipped a beat, I didn't completely lose all sense of self control like I usually did around him. "Close your eyes," he said, laughter in his eyes while I tried to catch my breath.

We were nearly on the other side of the observatory, and I could see the hill sloping downward just beneath where he'd set up my easel. "Why?" I asked, trying to find the answer in his grin.

"Just trust me," he said, and then he pressed his palm to my eyes.

I fervently prayed I wasn't wrong about him.

Leading me with his free hand, Luke brought me the rest of the way and helped me sit on a rock. The late afternoon sun warmed my skin, and the fresh smells of the trees and bushes filled my nose, and birds called to each other through the trees. Luke's hand was surprisingly soft, and I noted he smelled slightly of cucumbers. Weird.

"You ready?" he asked.

"I guess so," I replied.

I definitely wasn't ready. As Luke pulled his hand away and let me see what he'd kept so carefully hidden, I yet again lost the ability to breathe. But for a very different reason. I'd never seen anything like it, not in person. The golden hills rolled out from where I sat, soft in the sunlight and practically endless. A glittering stream wove through them, leaving a trail of lush trees in its path, and the sky settled above it all, bluer than I'd ever seen it. And beyond it all lay the coast, as if the city no longer existed, and the water stretched out until it met the sky in a shimmering line.

It was like I had left the California I knew behind and entered a whole different world.

I could feel Luke's eyes on me, but I couldn't get myself to look away from the expanse before me. I had no idea the world could look that beautiful, and yet there it was. Right in front of me. Daring me to become a part of it.

"That feeling," Luke whispered. "That's what you want to paint." And he placed a brush in my hand.

And oh did I paint. I was barely aware of what I was doing, but I painted until my back ached from hunching over the canvas. I painted until my fingers were stiff and my eyes burned from concentrating so hard. I painted until I was absolutely exhausted, and the sun touched the horizon ahead. It was like someone else had taken over my body, someone who knew exactly what she was doing and understood how to capture the way the expanse before me held an emotion I would never be able to put to words if I tried. It wasn't just copying what I saw, like I had done this morning. It was… I painted like my soul was fighting to be free of my body and become a part of the world in front of me, and I just had to keep going until I could breathe again.

And when I was finished, I sat and stared at the canvas, because I wasn't entirely sure what I'd just done.

It wasn't perfect. It almost looked nothing like the actual view, though I could see its inspirations. I'd gone with a darker feel. A wilder feel. And yet the whole thing had an overwhelming sense of peace to it, like if I could just get to the place I painted I wouldn't have any doubts or fears. I'd be home.

"I told you," Luke said, and this time his voice didn't startle me even though he'd been silent for hours.

I looked over to where he sat in the dirt, his back against a boulder and his grin both smug and kind. I couldn't even think of an argument, so I stretched my back and smiled. "That felt really good," I admitted. "Cathartic. Thank you."

The sky continued to golden as the sun sank lower, and though I wished I could stay there forever, I knew I should get back before I was missed. I started packing away my supplies, and Luke jumped up to help me. The whole afternoon felt like a dream, and reality hit me hard with every tube of paint I slipped into my bag. The sunset was a countdown. The quiet woods loudly told me I had to leave.

"How did you know about this place?" I asked to fill the silence.

Resting the easel over his shoulder and picking up my bag, Luke led the way back to the truck. "I used to come here all the time as a kid," he said. "Rode my bike up, and I'd just sit up here all night long looking at the stars."

Stars. While he tossed everything in the truck bed, I turned back to the abandoned observatory. "The stars must be amazing up here," I said, deeply envious of his childhood. My mother still never let me stay up past ten, and even lately she'd been checking on me to make sure I got my 'beauty sleep.' According to her, I needed all the help I could get.

Luke's eyes burned into my shoulders, and I turned just in time to catch an expression he quickly hid. Was he annoyed? But he covered it with a smile and folded his arms as he leaned against the truck. "We'll have to get you back up here so you can see them," he said and winked.

His use of the word 'we' sent a shiver through me.

"We should go," I said quickly.

His smile turned more playful, which made walking slightly more difficult. "Gotta get Cinderella back before midnight," he teased as he opened my door for me.

Neither of us said much on the drive back, which I didn't mind. Dusk was too peaceful for talking, so I held my painting in my lap and spent the whole drive smiling.

CHAPTER FOUR

"Lanna, you'll never guess what's happened!" Apparently we had progressed to bringing out the crazy before I even woke up, since my mother's exclamation pulled me out of what I thought was a nice dream. The details dissolved quickly, but I was pretty sure there was a dark-eyed gardener involved.

Tangled up in my blankets and barely awake, I looked up to find my mother sitting at the foot of my bed with her phone in hand. "What time is it?" I mumbled.

"Not early enough," she replied. "Not if we're going to have time to go shopping."

I sincerely hoped I was still dreaming. "Shopping? On a Sunday?" The stores would be madness as our entire social circle set out on the usual weekend hunt before brunch.

"Of course! You have absolutely no suitable sundresses."

I glanced toward my closet, where a pile of a good dozen sundresses sat heaped and discarded. She'd already gone through my clothes before even waking me up. Still bleary eyed, I tried my best to make sure she understood my expression. She was absolutely crazy. No doubt about that.

Just behind her on the dresser rested my painting from yesterday, and though I tried not to focus on it, I couldn't help but smile at the rolling hills and the glittering ocean and the trees that seemed to hide secrets, secrets I was desperate to learn. I'd painted that. The emotion that built up in my chest at the sight of it, the sense of peace and excitement and freedom, that had been me. If I had known I was capable of painting something like that, I would have painted in every free moment of every day.

But I couldn't focus on that, not when my mother sat there with crazed eyes and a little too much eagerness for me to be comfortable about this situation.

"Why do I need a sundress?" I asked finally.

Her already big eyes got even bigger as she held her phone toward me. "We've been invited!" she practically squealed.

I was half tempted to cover my ears. "To what?" I asked mid-yawn.

"To a garden party!"

We went to garden parties all the time. Something about this one was different. Or if it wasn't, she was going to get an earful about waking me up before breakfast was even ready. "And?" I prodded. "What's so special about it?"

She beamed from ear to ear, which was more terrifying than I thought she realized. "It's being hosted by Gilroy Munroe."

Ah. I failed to fight another yawn, even though she was literally bouncing with excitement. "How many favors did you have to pull to get that invite?" I muttered.

"Oh shush," she replied, not even the least bit discouraged. "What matters is now you can talk to Aaron without that Kennedy girl getting in your way!"

His name is Adam, I wanted to say, but I knew it wouldn't make a difference. She didn't care what his name was, just that he was rich and well connected.

"I saw how the two of you got along the other night," my mother continued, pulling at my covers in an effort to get me out of bed.

True, Adam had surprised me and wasn't as much a jerk as the rest of them. But anyone could pretend to be something they weren't; I was proof of that. At least on the rare occasions I actually did as I was told. I didn't hold out much hope for the Prince of Art, however, no matter what my mother thought she saw. Besides, our whole conversation had only been a couple minutes, so there was little chance she had actually seen anything promising. "Do I have to go?" I moaned, sitting up.

My question broke through her carefully positive attitude, and her claws gripped my leg, tight even through the blankets. "Lanna," she said in a huff, "you can't just spend all your days throwing paint at things! This could be your only chance unless you want to end up—"

"A poor, pathetic prostitute," I finished for her, though she'd never specifically used that term. "I'm not completely hopeless, you know. I don't need all your money." Even as I said it I squirmed a little, since I definitely did need money unless I wanted to be living out of a cardboard box.

She gritted her teeth, doing her very best to stay calm. Her effort *was* pretty impressive, but I worried I would one day push her too far and discover just how crazy the woman could get. "Lanna," she said again. "You only say that because you don't know what it's like to live without money."

"And you do?" I countered. "You grew up in Beverly Hills and have never worked a day in your life."

Brushing my comment away, she sighed and stretched across the bed to take my hand. The gesture was uncommonly gentle, which caught me off guard. "Please," she said softly. "I just want you to try. There's only so much I can do for you, and…"

Even if she didn't finish that sentence, I felt how much she truly cared about me. Despite the insults and the criticism and the complete lack of faith, she still treated me as her daughter. Most of the time. She really just wanted the best for me, and I wasn't sure if I could fault her for that. There were worse things she could do.

Taking a deep breath and letting it out slowly, I weighed my options. A mother could only have so much patience, and eventually she would give up if I kept fighting her. Or I could genuinely give Adam a chance. If he turned out to be like all the others, I could easily walk away and start planning my homeless life.

"Fine," I said before my mother fell apart. "I'll try. But you can't be part of it."

"Of course," she agreed far too quickly.

"I mean it," I told her. "You have to let me be me."

"But—"

"It's never going to work if I can't be myself," I argued.

She nodded, but her eyes flickered over to the pile of apparently worthless dresses on my floor. "Lanna…"

I was pretty sure that was an argument I couldn't win, even if I tried. "Fine," I said again. "We can go shopping. Give me twenty minutes."

"You have ten," she replied and snapped to her feet, suddenly back to her usual stiff self. I had the horrible impression as she strode out of the room that she had adopted that softer side just to get me to agree to her terms, and I felt like I hadn't won anything at all.

At that moment I caught the sounds of a lawn mower outside, and I fell back onto my pillows. It was going to be a long day.

* * *

Decked out in a brand new dress—one a whole lot shorter and pinker than I would have liked—I reluctantly agreed to take the town car, since the Munroes lived on the other side of town and there was no way we could walk that far. My mother sighed with exasperation as I trembled and strangled my seatbelt with my fingers, but we arrived without incident.

I stumbled out of the car the second our driver shut off the engine. Stumbled in the literal sense. I very nearly tripped face first into a large fern, silently cursing the existence of heels and only catching myself at the last possible second.

"Oh Lanna," my mother sighed behind me.

We followed the meticulously groomed rock path through a grove of trees south of the house, and I did my best to keep my stomach from churning. I had no need to be nervous. I'd been to so many garden parties that I couldn't even count them, and they all generally ended up the same way: me embarrassed by my own deficiencies and my mother completely disappointed. I'd gotten used to that part. So why did I feel so dizzy as the pathway brought me closer and closer to Adam Munroe?

"Here we are!" my mother announced, and I stopped dead.

'Here' was a halfway put together setup of tables and chairs and three very confused caterers who were only beginning to unload their food. Feeling suddenly dizzy, I stared at my mother's grin and tried to understand how I could be so normal compared to her. She was certifiably insane.

"I can't believe you," I groaned, and if I didn't know she sent the car away as soon as we got out, I would have marched straight back and refused to stay. But no, she planned for us to get there ridiculously early, probably to give me extra time with Adam without any other guests getting in the way.

"Lanna?" asked a soft voice behind us.

I turned slowly, knowing I probably looked horribly red. I certainly felt the heat. "Adam," I greeted, and my voice cracked. *Awesome.* "Sorry, I didn't realize we would be here so early."

His blue eyes flicked over to my mother, who still looked way too proud of herself as she pretended to admire the grounds. Would he understand it wasn't my fault? Would he rescind the invitation? I half hoped he would decide I was just as scheming as her, because that would give me an inarguable reason to give up on all of this. If he saw me just like the other girls who went after him, I stood no chance.

"It's fine," he said after an uncomfortably long period of silence. Not a man of many words apparently. Compared to Chandler Wixcomb, who could spend hours going on and on about his precious horses, it was almost refreshing to meet a man who didn't feel the need to talk.

"I'm really sorry," I repeated. "Do you maybe have a place we can sit and wait? I don't want to be in the way." I grabbed my mother's arm before she could try to argue, and I watched Adam's dark eyes follow the movement.

"Of course," he replied. With a nod of his head indicating he wanted us to follow, he led the way.

Though the caterers still gave us wary glances, at least Adam didn't seem completely off put. For some reason, knowing that gave me a lot of relief, and I relaxed a little as we crossed the Munroes' perfect lawn. At least until my mother decided to open her mouth.

"How long has your family lived here, Mr. Munroe?" she asked, thankfully not calling him Aaron. Her voice wobbled as she did, since she'd been adamant about wearing stiletto heels despite knowing the party would take place outside and in the grass. She kept sinking deep and having to pull herself free.

"Ten years," Adam replied.

That was surprising. Most of the wealthy families had owned their land for ages. I didn't know much about the Munroe family aside from Gilroy's art expertise, but maybe they came from newer money than I'd imagined. Maybe that was why I'd never met Adam before.

"How much is the house worth?" my mother asked, and my stomach dropped.

My face burned when Adam slowed enough to look at her, and I knew for sure he would turn cold and ask us to leave. It was one thing to brag about her own money, but asking about his? That was horrible.

But Adam smiled briefly and gestured his arm to an ornate metal bench that sat beneath a canopy of trees. "I'm not sure," he replied smoothly. "Dad just did a bunch of remodeling, so I'm sure it's changed."

I sat at the very edge of the bench—my dress was seriously too short—and tried not to stare at Adam with my mouth agape. Not many people could combat my mother that well. And to my even further surprise, Adam sat next to me, leaving her to take a seat on his other side.

Adam suddenly leaned closer to me and softly said, "I hope it isn't too cold in the shade. It's pretty cool out this morning."

I glanced at the goosebumps on my arms, not entirely sure they were from the cold. He smelled vaguely of fresh oranges, and with him this close I realized his dark hair was damp, as if he'd only recently showered. Now that he wasn't in a tux—just dark jeans and a light blue button up shirt with the sleeves rolled up to his elbows—he didn't look as stiff as I remembered him from the other night.

My mother coughed once, and I blinked as my cheeks burned yet again. *Stop staring at The Prince.* "I'll be fine," I assured Adam, and he smiled a little. "So where did you grow up, then, if not here?"

"I think I'll walk along this lovely stream for a bit," my mother declared suddenly. Though she continued to sink into the soft ground, she maintained her high head and wandered off through the little grove of trees that lined the property, much to my consternation. Did she actually trust me to have a conversation on my own? I never thought it was possible.

Adam waited until she was out of earshot, and then he dropped his elbows to his knees and let out a sigh. "Sorry," he murmured to the ground. "I know you probably don't want to be here."

I hadn't expected that, and I stared at him for a second before I found my voice again. "What makes you say that?" I asked. Especially because the longer I sat here, the more I was realizing I was totally okay with the circumstances. There was something intriguing about Adam, though I couldn't quite place what it was.

He didn't even look at me. "My dad. He, uh, he seems to think I need a partner in life as soon as possible. Just like your mom does for you. So… So I know how it feels to be paraded around."

"Yeah," I replied, mostly because I didn't have a better response. No wonder he wasn't giving those ladies any attention at the gala the other night. Unlike the rest of our world, he wasn't on the hunt.

"Do you ever just…" He paused, taking in a deep breath then letting it out slowly. Sitting up again, he turned to me and gave me a smile that didn't quite reach his eyes. I wondered what he would look like if he really did smile. He was already pretty breathtaking, definitely in the royal category, but he didn't look happy. And happiness on a man's face made him look more handsome than any jawline or haircut. I was convinced it was impossible to know a person until you'd seen them really smile.

"I have an idea," he said, obviously changing his mind about what he wanted to say. "We both have to get through this party, right?"

I wasn't sure where he was going with that, but I nodded. "Right."

"And I have a feeling you aren't all that interested in being forced to socialize with all those…"

"Sycophants?" I supplied with a smile.

He chuckled, his smile still only half there. "Exactly."

"So what are you proposing?" I asked, knowing full well my mother intended to keep me by Adam's side no matter what.

He took another deep breath, and I had the sudden feeling Adam Munroe was a reasonably shy individual. I wouldn't have guessed it looking at him—and I certainly found it hard to look away—but he was nervous. Nervous about the party, and nervous about what he was going to ask me.

"I wondered," he said slowly, "if you would be interested in being my date today." Did people have dates at garden parties? Whatever my face was doing, Adam obviously took it the wrong way and blushed a little pink as his eyes fell back to the ground at his feet. "Of course not," he mumbled. "That's stupid."

"No!" I said quickly, and I even put my hand on his arm to make sure he understood my sincerity. My mother would kill me if she knew I'd accidentally embarrassed my future husband—her words, not mine. "No, I think that's a great idea. I'd definitely rather talk to you than…than anyone, really."

Adam's relieved smile very nearly lit up his eyes, and even if it wasn't full happiness, my heart skipped a beat at the sight. "Really?" he asked, almost as if he couldn't fathom the idea of someone wanting to spend time with him. "That's… Thank you, Lanna. You might make today bearable."

I definitely blushed at that, realizing a second later I still had my hand on his arm. And that I enjoyed touching him more than I would have guessed. And that my mother was stumbling back our way. Pulling my hand back, I gave Adam a quick smile and tried to find a conversation so my mother wouldn't think we'd been sitting there in silence the whole time. She would skin me alive.

"Does your father host a lot of these parties?" I asked.

He shrugged, his eyes also on the approaching woman in heels. "He didn't until recently. Dad doesn't love parties, but…"

"But it's the best way to get you out in society," I finished for him. "I understand that well. But what made him decide to start?"

Adam's ears suddenly turned red, and he was back to leaning on his knees and speaking to the ground. "I, uh, I broke up with my fiancée," he said, almost too quietly for me to even hear him. "Several months ago."

Why did that disappoint me so much? I found myself scooting a half inch away, my smile completely fake. Luckily I'd had a lot of practice pretending to be happy. "I'm sorry. What happened?" Not that this was a conversation I wanted my mother to be a part of, but I couldn't help asking.

Adam simply shrugged then looked up. "Mrs. Davenport," he greeted, his smile as unreal as mine. "How was your walk?"

Mud caked her shoes, but her wide grin made it seem like she wouldn't actually blame the mess on me. Not that I really believed that. *The things I do for you,* I could imagine her saying. "Oh, it was just what I needed," she replied sweetly. "I noticed a couple guests have arrived," she continued then practically glided away toward the party, much too pleased with herself.

I sighed, not bothering to hide it. "She's going to be the death of me," I groaned.

Slowly rising, Adam took a moment to assume his princely facade, and then he reached out for my hand. "Let's just try to make it through today," he said. "Together."

* * *

Not that I'd ever considered myself very well liked, but after an hour of receiving glare after glare, even from some of the men in attendance, I decided I had taken my overlooked existence for granted. I had no idea people could make such disgusted expressions while simultaneously whispering to each other, and every negative comment seemed directed right at me and the fact that I had managed to claim the attention of the Prince of Art. And all the while my mother beamed and simpered like she was having the best day of her life.

Adam and I never really left each other's side. Through some unspoken agreement, we either linked arms or clasped hands or sat shoulder to shoulder, even if we were talking to separate guests. Most of the time I just stood at his side and let him talk. When forced, the man really knew how to hold a conversation, and I envied him for it. Sometimes he would pull me in to the conversation, but if he noticed me fumbling for something to say he deftly changed the subject or greeted another guest. For someone who hadn't been attending many functions, he certainly knew a lot of people.

I was in the middle of downing a cup of punch—the sun beat down a lot warmer when you were under pressure—when Adam's voice hit me hard: "Lanna, I'd like you to meet my father."

I choked, spewing punch all over Margaret Taft and the Yorkie she always carried with her. "Sorry," I gasped over her outrage. Adam steadied me, patting my back gently until I stopped coughing, and then I turned with red face and watering eyes to one of my idols. "Mr. Munroe," I said between a couple more coughs. "It's an honor."

The King of Art offered me a slight nod instead of a handshake, and his eyes followed Margaret as she hurried off to clean up herself and her dog, Mr. Tufty. He looked very much like Adam, tall and solid, though his thick dark hair was peppered with gray and his eyes were brown instead of blue. I had always imagined him to be an older guy, balding and porky and with an impressively bushy mustache, though I had no idea why. But he was likely younger than my father, even if he looked a little more worn than him, and he was just as handsome as his son. "Miss Davenport," he said, his voice deep and husky. "My son tells me you appreciate art. Have you studied it much?"

Should I curtsy? I should curtsy. But Adam slipped his fingers between mine before I could, which was probably a good idea. "Um." Why couldn't I remember how to speak? "Yeah. A little. I mean, I mostly just paint on my own, so…" I shut my mouth, wishing I could just vanish and pretend I didn't sound absolutely pathetic.

Munroe didn't look impressed, and his eyes held a little too long on my hand entwined with his son's. For the first time I wanted to pull away from Adam, but he held strong. "You paint?" Munroe replied, raising one eyebrow. "Do you have anything in the galleries in town I might have seen?"

Ha! I would die of shame if a man of his caliber ever saw one of my paintings, and it wasn't like I would ever let anyone see my paintings, except maybe a gardener or two. Well, only the one. "Um. Not yet. Maybe someday." *Or never.*

"She paints beautifully," Adam said suddenly, and I turned my head to stare up at him. Why would he say something like that when he'd obviously never seen my paintings? The man had only met me two days ago, for crying out loud! "She definitely has a real talent," Adam continued. "I plan to keep an eye on her before someone else discovers what she can do."

Not that I was the picture of honesty with my mother, but did he just lie flat out to his own father? My face burned even hotter beneath the sun, and I started to feel a bit dizzy. I didn't know what was going on, and I very much hoped Adam would explain it to me before the whole world thought I was something I wasn't.

"Huh," Munroe replied. "I'll have to see one of these masterpieces of yours, Miss Davenport. If you'll excuse me." He nodded once more then crossed the lawn to speak to a rough-looking man who hovered at the edge of the party. Whoever he was, he certainly didn't fit in with the rest of the guests in his t-shirt and jeans and looked thoroughly uncomfortable, as if he knew his contrast well. He and Munroe strode behind a hedge and disappeared. Strange, that Mr. Munroe would leave his own party…

"Lanna, are you okay?" Adam's question punctuated my dizziness, and my knees gave out. He slipped an arm around my waist and clasped my elbow, and his citrus scent nearly overwhelmed me. "Here, come sit down." I was barely aware of him leading me to a stray chair that sat in some shade beneath one of the temporary canopies, but when he pressed a cool hand to my cheek, I couldn't acknowledge anyone but him. Were they staring at me? Probably. "You're really warm," Adam said, and the concern in his voice made it deeper. Stronger.

"I'm fine," I assured him, but my voice came out breathy and weak. The complete opposite of his. "It's just the sun. And…"

"And what I said to my dad," he guessed as he crouched in front of me.

Shrugging, I pressed my fingers to my aching temples. "Why did you say it?" I asked, trying not to sound accusing. "I mean, it was very kind, but you haven't…"

"I haven't seen your work," he admitted. His eyes traced my face, his thick eyebrows pulled together with worry. "I have a feeling, though," he continued softly. "You know exactly what it means to paint your soul into something."

I'm working on that, I couldn't help but think.

"Lanna, are you sure you're okay? You look…" He didn't even have a word for it, which made me feel awesome.

I glanced over at the rest of the party, where a couple dozen people watched us—me, in particular—with annoyance and frustration. I had a feeling more than one person had come to this garden to meet the mysterious Prince, and here I was tearing him away from their chance to rub shoulders with royalty. Gilroy Munroe was one thing. The eligible heir apparent was another entirely. There were mothers in that crowd. Fathers. Women who didn't realize their age and sought conquest wherever they could.

And crouched in front of me, his hand on my bare knee and his eyes so intently focused that not even a call of his name drew his attention away, was the most eligible bachelor in the state.

Compared to him I was nothing. Compared to every other person waiting just a few steps away, I was completely insignificant. No matter how much I liked holding his hand, no matter how easy it was to want to stay at his side and watch him play his part, I was no good for him. Surely he could see that as well as the rest of the world.

"I should probably go home," I said, a little bit shocked by how hard it was to say. "And you should get back to your guests."

His hand dropped from my knee almost immediately. "Oh. Yeah, that's probably…" He shut his jaw tight and stood, and he almost looked angry. At me? Or something else? "I'll…" He held out his arm without finishing his sentence, and I understood. He would walk me to the car like any good gentleman should, and then we would never have to interact again.

It was better that way, I told myself.

Even if I didn't believe it.

CHAPTER FIVE

"That is the saddest daffodil I have ever seen." Somehow Luke's words didn't frighten me, and in a strange way I didn't like it. There was something refreshing about the adrenaline of completely losing all sense of control, if only for a moment, and that wasn't there. At all.

"And I mean that in the emotional sense, not the artistic sense," he continued. "It's actually very well done."

I hadn't had the energy to pull out my paints, but something in me had absolutely needed to put something on a page before my thoughts overwhelmed me. Though my mother tried her best to convince me to go into town with her and lay waste to the boutiques after lunch, I'd grabbed my sketchbook and gone back to the pond and plopped down in the grass with my charcoal. I'd only been lying there on my stomach and sketching one of the few daffodils there at the edge of the pond for an hour before Luke found me like he always did.

Setting his rake against the side of the bench, the gardener stretched himself out on his back next to me, his arms behind his head and his mischievous smile in place as he looked up at me. "So why the drawing?" he asked. "I thought painting was, you know, your thing."

"You know nothing about me," I mumbled back and immediately regretted my bitter tone. I wasn't angry with him. I was angry with myself. Why? I didn't know.

Luckily, he didn't deflate and lightly replied, "Maybe. Why do you think I keep coming back to the Davenport Castle?"

"You work here," I pointed out, deciding not to comment on the castle comparison. It was more like a dungeon, anyway, especially now that I knew there was more out there than parties with the rich snobs. There were golden hills and princes who acted nothing like I expected them to.

Luke's smile widened a little. "Why do you think I took the job?"

As he probably knew they would, my cheeks burned red. I pressed a hand to the one nearest him, hoping to hide it by pretending to rest my chin in my palm. "I just felt like sketching," I said after a moment. "It better fit the mood."

He rolled over, his shoulder knocking into mine as he gazed at my drawing again. "And why are we depressed today, Princess?" He asked the question so nonchalantly that I wasn't sure he meant it. Not until his eyes met mine and I could see his sincerity.

Did I really want to tell him? Talking about painting was one thing, but sharing my disappointments from yesterday was another. Honestly, I wanted to forget the garden party had even happened, mainly because I knew it wouldn't happen again. Still, when I'd told him about when Ben died, I had actually felt a bit better about the whole thing. Maybe talking through my problems and emotions was a good thing, and there was something about Luke Hawthorne's easy nature and unassuming questions that made me want to tell him everything.

"I went to this party yesterday," I started before I could stop myself. I needed *someone* to help me figure out why I felt this way.

Luke nodded. "At the Munroe place," he confirmed.

I stared at him.

He just shrugged and said, "People talk," before gesturing for me to continue.

"And my insane mother brought me there half an hour early, before the party even started. It was her way of getting me to talk to Adam Munroe before anyone else could."

Half smiling, Luke played with a blade of grass and muttered, "She sounds diabolical."

"You have no idea," I replied.

"So she's trying to play matchmaker with you and the Prince of Art. People talk," he repeated before I could question his knowledge of the wealthy world. "And how did it go?" he pressed.

Sighing, I added a few unnecessary details to my daffodil drawing. "He was…" How could I even describe Adam? Every time I thought I knew what to expect from him, he turned around and surprised me. Granted, I'd only met him twice, but usually I learned as much as I needed to know about an elite within the first five minutes of meeting them, since they were all the same. Adam Munroe was something different.

"Boring?" Luke tried, and I couldn't help but laugh at his raised eyebrow. "Stupid? Absolutely pompous?"

"Thoughtful," I countered before he came up with anything more colorful. "Refreshing."

"So naturally you had to draw a flower that makes me want to cry just by looking at it."

Bumping his shoulder with mine, I rolled my eyes and said, "Are you going to let me talk or not? I'm trying to bare my soul here."

Looking fully repentant—an expression I hadn't really expected someone like Luke to be capable of—he pursed his lips shut and rolled over onto his side, his head in his hand and light dancing in his dark eyes. "Bare away," he said gently.

How would I even put it into words? "I don't know," I said. "I expected him to be like all the others. Full of himself. Stuck up. Superior. That's how millionaires act."

"Not all of them," Luke muttered, mostly to himself.

Ignoring the comment, I continued: "He was actually human. Just as uncomfortable as I was, and somehow he seemed to recognize that I didn't want to be there anymore than he did. I don't know how he did it, but he figured out a way to make the party actually interesting, and he didn't treat me like the rest of them do. He didn't see an awkward, clumsy girl who would rather paint in a stable than put on makeup and curl her hair. He was actually nice to me. More than nice. He was…" Something I couldn't describe.

His gaze on the grass he spun between his fingers, Luke barely seemed to breathe as he lay there next to me. "So what's the problem?" he asked quietly. "He seems like a good match. Rich, handsome, intelligent…"

I didn't even have to think about that question. "The problem is I'm an awkward, clumsy girl who would rather paint in a stable than put on makeup and curl her hair. I constantly have paint on my clothes and charcoal on my fingers and I can't even take a drink without spitting it on Mr. Tufty."

Luke's eyes jumped up to mine, and his unspoken question played at his lips.

"Don't ask," I replied. I didn't particularly want to relive that moment of the day. Margaret Taft would probably avoid me like the plague for the rest of my life.

"So you don't think you're in the same league as the handsome prince," he said. As usual, he was way more observant than he should have been, and his eyes seemed to read so much in my face. "I hate to break it to you, Princess, but I'm pretty sure *he's* not in *your* league, and he knows it."

"Ha," I said, slowly sitting up and rounding out my stiff back. "I'm serious, Luke."

"So am I," he replied as he followed me up. "If Adam Munroe has any sense, he won't let you get very far."

We sat nearly hip to hip, but the closeness didn't bother me. We just sat there watching each other, and I wondered how we had suddenly become friends. It was like I'd known him for years, like I knew his every quirk and flaw, though I couldn't put a name to them. Something about this gardener made me want to forget everything my mother ever taught me and just figure out who I was. What my own quirks and flaws were.

I had always wanted a best friend, and maybe…

My phone buzzed suddenly, sending my heart pounding as I jumped because my phone rarely rang. The only reason I even had it was so my mother could call me back to the house if she thought I'd spent too much time out in the yard. Luke laughed despite my glare, and though I didn't recognize the number, I answered anyway, covering Luke's mouth to keep him quiet.

"Hello?"

"Lanna?" asked the deep voice on the other end.

I sat up straighter. "Adam? What are—"

"I wanted to make sure you were feeling better," he interrupted, catching me off guard. "And to ask if you wanted to come to a, um, party we're having tomorrow night."

"A party?" I repeated, completely confused. Why would he want me at yet another party?

Luke raised his eyebrows at me, and I realized I still had my hand over his mouth. I pulled it away slowly.

"Yes," Adam replied. "We're celebrating a new acquisition. A Renoir."

"Wait, you have a Renoir? Seriously?"

Adam laughed, and immediately my face burned. "I thought you might like to see it," he said. So he invited me for the art. That made sense. A lot more sense than him actually wanting me to come for the party itself. After my punch display with Margaret and her dog, I was pretty sure not even my mother could get me invitations to the fancy events anymore.

"What sweet nothings is your pretty prince telling you?" Luke asked suddenly.

I stared at him and prayed Adam didn't hear. "That sounds amazing," I told Adam and gave Luke a glare that made him grin.

"Plus," Adam added, suddenly quieter, "the whole thing would probably be a lot better with you there, so…"

Suddenly I wished Luke wasn't sitting there watching me, because his eyes traced the blush on my cheeks as I tried to keep my voice steady. Maybe I was wrong. Maybe I wasn't completely hopeless. Even if Adam just wanted me there as a friend, something to help him weather the winds of the rich and powerful, it sounded like he actually liked me. For who I was, not who I was supposed to be. That was a new feeling.

Turning my back to the gardener, I pressed my phone a little closer to my ear and couldn't help but smile as I said, "I would love to come."

I thought I heard his sigh of relief, which only broadened my grin. "Great," he said. "I'll, uh, make sure you're on the list, and I'll text you the details."

"Wait," I said.

He sounded hesitant: "Yeah?"

"You're not inviting my mother, are you?"

"Do…do you want me to?"

"Of course not," I replied.

"Then she's not invited. I'll see you tomorrow, Lanna."

"See you," I whispered back and hung up.

"So he invited you to a party?" Luke said loudly.

I jumped and spun around, my eyes wide and my heart racing. Honestly, how did he even *do* that so well?

Though he smiled, Luke didn't look particularly happy. I glanced at my daffodil sketch and didn't like the similarities between them. "I see how it is," he continued, his voice not nearly as light as usual. "You hear the silky voice of the great Adam Munroe and forget I'm even here."

I frowned. "That's not—"

"I get it," he interrupted, his hands in the air in surrender. "Not many can compete with a man of his caliber."

"Do…" I wasn't sure how to ask my question. "Are you trying to compete?"

He kept his eyes on me, his expression completely unreadable. But only for a moment, and then everything softened as he brought his smile back and leaned back on his hands. "Eh," he said, "I'm not sure I'd have a chance even if I was."

What kind of an answer was that?

"An-y-way," Luke continued, drawing out the syllables. "Does that mean I don't have to look at any more depressing flowers now that your prince hasn't abandoned you? You seem happier already."

I was. Happier. Wasn't I?

Rising to his feet, Luke stretched wide then helped me up. "I have to get back to work," he said, "but I'm glad you're not so down in the dumps." Then he reached down and plucked the daffodil I'd used as inspiration for my sketch, holding it out to me.

"I'm pretty sure you weren't supposed to do that," I said, though I took the flower anyway.

He just shrugged, said, "I'll plant another," and then he wandered off across the lawn.

* * *

"Um." I stood in the doorway of my father's home office, not entirely sure what I was doing there. I'd been walking through the house lost in thought until I was suddenly knocking on his open door. "Do you have a second? To talk?"

He'd been reading something on his computer, but he looked over at me. At least I thought he did. It was hard to tell with the screen adding a glare to his reading glasses. "Lanna?" So he found this strange too. At least it wasn't just me. "Is something wrong? You did seem a bit off at dinner."

Honestly, I was surprised he noticed. On the rare occasions he actually took the time to sit and eat with my mother and me, my father generally had a newspaper or his phone in hand and stayed just long enough to absently eat whatever it was our chef Shelly cooked for us. Most of the time, if he didn't order takeout to his desk, he ate on the way home from his office in the city.

"Nothing's…wrong," I replied. I felt thirteen again, nervous and awkward and not completely sure if my father had any idea what was going on in his daughter's life. "I just wanted to ask you something."

"About?"

"Adam Munroe."

He looked at me for a second, his eyebrows pulled together not in anger but in concentration. Then he clicked his screen off and rose to his feet. "Do you want to sit?" he asked, gesturing to the two armchairs that sat angled in front of his wall of books.

My father was a lot like me. Quiet, independent, opinionated, more on the shy side. It had taken a lot of imagination when I was younger to picture the corporate lawyer that he was, but after I got a chance to see him in action when I was about sixteen, I definitely understood why he was in such high demand. When the man took a stand and put his energy into something, he could be terrifying without even raising his voice. It was all in his gaze, in the way he looked at a person like they were insignificant and disposable.

As I sat next to him, I desperately prayed I would never, ever see that side of my father at home. If this conversation turned a way I didn't want it to go, the risk of seeing his cold lawyer side was certainly there, and I wanted to make sure I kept control of the topic.

"So what is this about, specifically?" he asked, and luckily his voice was soft. Tired, almost, which hopefully meant he didn't have the energy to go too deep into the chat.

"Well…" I hadn't exactly planned on going to his home office, so I definitely hadn't figured out what I would say. "I know Mr. Munroe is your client, but do you know him very well?"

He pursed his lips, probably trying to figure out my purpose for the conversation. "You mean Gilroy? We've been friends for a few years now."

I wasn't sure my father *had* friends, not in the normal sense of the word, but his response did offer just a little bit of insight. "Have you ever met his son?"

"A few times," he replied. "Quiet kid, but he's nice enough." That wasn't much to go on. I trusted my father's opinion of people, since it was often his job to know a man's motives and intentions, but I wanted to get some insight into 'The Prince.' Try to figure out who he was before I let myself trust him too much. "Knows business like the back of his hand, though," my father continued suddenly. "Give him a year, and he'll be running all of Munroe Royalties and then some."

"He knows business?" I repeated. "But art dealing…that's an intense thing. It takes someone who can hold strong or push harder to get a good sell."

"Exactly," Father replied. "Gilroy just purchased a new painting, something famous, and you should have seen the kid at work. Completely cutthroat."

Cutthroat? Adam? I'd seen a lot of sides to him, but I never would have called him anything but kind. Not after meeting him. "I didn't know that," I said quietly. Was the Adam I saw at the garden party a mask? Or was the hardened businessman the facade? It was hard to know, and I sat there in my father's study more confused than when I walked in.

"You like him?" he asked, a little too knowingly. I had a feeling he could read a lot more in my face than I realized.

"Maybe," I replied honestly. "I'm not sure I know him all that well. But he seems better than the others."

"The others are idiots," my father agreed, bringing a smile to my face. "I may have been born to privilege, but I don't parade it around like the rest of them."

"So you're not mad every time I turn down one of Mother's prospects?" I'd never really considered how my father felt about the whole matchmaking thing. Not seriously. He never seemed to bother paying attention, so I didn't know how much he actually knew.

He smiled and touched a gentle hand to my arm. "My dear Lanna, you are my princess." Bad choice of words, but I put that aside and listened eagerly. "I want to see you cared for, but I also want to see you happy. I don't see the need to force you into something that will only make you miserable."

"Your wife doesn't feel that way," I grumbled, even though I positively beamed with pleasure.

But my father only chuckled a little and got up to go back to his desk, silently telling me our conversation was over so he could get back to work. "Your mother cares for you as much as I do," he said. "Even if she doesn't know how to show it. Goodnight, Lanna."

"Goodnight, Father."

CHAPTER SIX

I left for the Munroes' party with hardly a minute to spare in order to get there on time. Mother spent a considerable amount of effort on my hair—"Honestly, Lanna, how do you *always* have paint in your hair?"—and lectured me on how to behave at a function like that. By the time I managed to get out the door and climb into the town car, I felt ready to give up and blame my timing on fate.

I spent the drive drawing in a little notebook I'd stuffed into my clutch. If I pretended I was at home in my room, the roads didn't terrify me quite as much, though that didn't stop my heart from trying to pound out of my chest. One day I would no longer be afraid to sit in a car, but it wasn't that day.

"Thanks, Stefan," I told my driver as he opened my door. "I'll probably be a couple hours." He nodded his understanding then drove off, leaving me looking up at the impressive facade of the Munroe mansion. The King of Art certainly had good taste, I noted. I also noted I was alone on the steps, no cars coming or going along the driveway. Either I was very early, or I was very late.

Adam's text did say eight, didn't it?

Before I could dig my phone out of my purse, the front door opened with a flash of light and sound. Shielding my eyes, I watched a silhouette draw nearer until it stood right in front of me. Weirdly, I didn't have to see him to know exactly who it was.

"Hi, Adam," I said and turned myself so I could actually see his face in the light.

He spent a moment taking me in, and then he smiled. Still that almost smile, but I decided to make it my goal to one day get that happiness to reach his eyes. As long as he kept me around, at least. The night would be a test of my ability to not completely make a fool of myself and embarrass Adam in the process.

"I'm glad you're here, Lanna," he said quietly. "Only…" I definitely didn't like the red in his face as he stood there, hesitant to say what was on his mind. "I, uh, made sure you would be the last one here."

My heart sank, thumping low in my chest. "Why would you do that?" I whispered. Inevitably people would notice when I walked in, so there was no way I could blend in with the crowd.

Adam reached out for my hand, which I surrendered reluctantly. The night felt suddenly cold, and I berated myself for sending Stefan away with the car.

"Don't be mad at me," Adam pleaded. The begging was a nice touch, not that it helped much. "I just thought… Maybe this was a bad idea," he admitted.

He was probably right, but… Too curious to let it go, I sighed. "What?"

He bowed his head, at least ashamed of his plan. "I thought if everyone saw you with me, they'd leave me alone. Give up the pursuit."

I actually laughed, though I probably shouldn't have. "You think I'd be enough to get the mothers off your back? You're right. Bad idea."

But he pulled his eyebrows together, looking at me with nothing but confusion. "Why wouldn't it work?" he asked.

The sincerity in his voice caught me off guard, and I stared up at him with my heart now in my throat. "I mean… Look at me." Paint in my hair, thoroughly uncomfortable in my heels and glittering dress, I had always stood out among my peers. If I could have worn jeans and a t-shirt, I would have. I wasn't proper or poised. I spit juice on people and tripped into bushes.

Adam pulled me the slightest bit closer, his blue eyes traveling my face as it burned hotter and hotter. "Exactly," he practically whispered.

Goodness, I had no idea a man could look at me like that, and for a moment I thought I might melt into the floor. Even if I was only there to save him from the crazies, he couldn't fake a look like that, and I felt beautiful for the first time ever.

"Okay," I breathed.

Adam's eyes sparkled, hinting at that happiness that lurked just beneath the surface. "I owe you one," he said, close enough that his breath brushed my hair and sent a shiver through me. "This way."

Adam led me inside, and I barely had time to take in the surprising coziness of the entryway before he pulled me down a side hall. "I need to check on something first, so if you wouldn't mind waiting here a minute…"

I gasped the moment I saw the row of paintings lining the wall of the hallway, barely registering Adam releasing my hand and disappearing. It was incredible! Gilroy Munroe's reputation for collecting exquisite art wasn't just rumor, and it seemed he had saved some of the best for his own home. He had some of the most incredible works I'd ever seen, and—

"No way," I said out loud as I paused in front of an impressionist painting that was famous enough for me to know the title just by looking at it. "He has a Seurat?"

"It's nice," a man replied, making me jump. "Isn't it?"

I turned to agree, but then I saw who leaned against a nearby wall and grinned at me like he'd just been watching the most amusing thing. How was he there? My heart kicking into double speed, I just stared at him until his smile softened and he said, "Hey, Lanna."

Then I marched up to him and slapped him across the cheek. "What the *hell*, Matthew?"

"Whoa!" he cried, stepping back and massaging the skin on his face. "Where did that come from?"

A good question, since I'd never slapped anyone before in my life, but I kept with my angry energy and replied, "You haven't come home in *years*. Not even a phone call. My own brother!"

His hand dropping, Matthew cringed and fought for an explanation.

I didn't let him find one. "The last time I saw you, you were so drunk you barely recognized me. I knew when you got back from the Army you'd be different, but you were a total stranger. You couldn't even smile, and…" When had I started crying? "And now look at you! You look…"

Suddenly I was in his arms, and he held me so tight it hurt. But I didn't care, and I pulled him even closer. I had been missing my brother, but I had no idea how bad it was until I had him there in my arms. It felt like a piece of me had just fallen back into place. "Better," he said into my hair. "I look better. Lanna, I'm so sorry."

The last decade came rushing back all at once. Benjamin's death, Matthew enlisting in the Army before he even graduated high school, me suddenly being completely alone. Matthew had always been the lighthearted one, the prankster, the one who kept us laughing until our sides hurt. After Ben died, something broke inside Matthew, and he spiraled until I hardly saw my brother in him anymore.

But looking at him there in the Munroes' house, the last place I would have expected to see him, it was like he'd never even changed. Sure, he was older and stronger, and he held himself more stiffly than he'd used to, but beneath his thick brown hair were the same gray-blue eyes that matched mine and seemed to dance with happiness, as if he were thinking of a terrific joke he couldn't wait to share. He was healthy and strong and full of life, and I suddenly had my brother back. And I had no idea how to handle it.

"Hey," he said gently and rubbed slow circles on my back. "Hey, Lawn Mower, it's okay."

I snorted at the old nickname, and that thankfully stopped my tears, though I worried my mother's painstaking makeup was now ruined. "I just…" I didn't even know how to put my emotions into words. "I'm so happy to see you, Matthew. The real you."

He grinned, and my knees went weak at the sight. I'd gone more than ten years without that silly lopsided smile, and I'd given up hope of ever seeing it again. Rubbing his thumbs under my eyes and attempting to fix my face, Matthew spoke with laughter in his words: "Mom's going to kill me if she finds out I messed this up," he said. "Lucky for you, I think she went with the waterproof variety."

"What are you doing here?" I asked. I gripped his arm, afraid that if I let go he'd disappear and that all of this would be a dream.

"Believe it or not, I work here."

"I don't believe it."

He laughed, and the sound carried down the hallway like it used to. "After I left the Army, I found myself in need of a job. I could have gone back home, but…" He frowned just a little, but not enough to dim his overall happiness. "I wasn't myself," he continued, "and I didn't want you to have to see me like that. Again."

"That doesn't explain what you're doing *here*," I pressed and took the handkerchief he offered me. My makeup might have been okay, but my nose was starting to make a mess.

"Vets make good bodyguards," he replied. His eyes focused on something behind me and lit up even more.

"Yes they do," Adam agreed behind me.

My eyes went wide, and I looked at Matthew in alarm. He just shook his head and smiled, letting me know I was presentable. Hoping my eyes weren't too red, I turned and gave Adam a smile.

He immediately slipped into the same expression he'd had at the garden party. "Are you okay, Lanna?" he asked and put his hand on my arm behind my elbow.

More than okay. I had my brother back. "I'm great," I said and really meant it. "Matthew works for you? As a…a bodyguard?"

His smile returning, Adam nodded and gave Matthew a pointed look. "For my father, more often. Art can be a dangerous business," he said.

"And I need to get back to it," Matthew replied. He quickly kissed the top of my head, said, "See you, Lawn Mower," and bounded off down the hall, full of energy.

"Lawn Mower?" Adam asked, one eyebrow raised.

I couldn't help but notice how especially attractive he was when he had that playfulness to him, and my breath caught a little in my throat. "My brother Ben gave me the nickname when he was twelve, and he and Matthew both thought it was hilarious. He hasn't called me that in years." Eleven, to be exact. Not since the funeral. "I'm a little mortified you know about it," I added.

"I think it's cute," Adam replied, and I was pretty sure he blushed more than I did. Coughing, he gestured back the way we came. "Are you ready for this?"

"Never," I said and took his arm. "Let's do this."

If I hadn't been riding high from seeing my brother alive and—I barely let myself believe it—*happy*, I definitely wouldn't have enjoyed our entrance into the Munroe gathering room. But thanks to the smiles of my wonderful older brother, I beamed as Adam led me inside. All conversation among the thirty or so in attendance stopped nearly instantaneously, and even though the music still played, the room was absolutely silent as all eyes turned to us.

"I'm really sorry," Adam muttered, leaning just the slightest bit closer to me as he walked.

"Don't be," I replied, and I meant it. "I'm pretty sure this will give me a little peace too. Especially from my mother."

And then the whispers started.

Adam led me straight through the parting crowd, and though he smiled, his arm was completely tense against mine. Those we passed weren't exactly quiet, and I was sure Adam heard like I did the comments people made to each other. *Those two? Where did she come from? He could do better. When did Davenport's princess grow up?*

That last one made me turn my head, and I caught the eye of a woman I had only met once or twice. Selena Pye. Unlike most of the older ladies, she didn't have any children to pawn off, so I hadn't paid her much attention. But she gave me a slight smile, an *earnest* smile, and my quickly growing nerves subsided almost entirely. The whole world wasn't completely against me, then. That was nice to know.

"Ignore everyone, Adam," I said as we reached the other side of the little ballroom and the whispers became a loud buzz behind us. "They're not worth your attention."

But when we stopped near his father, Adam shook his head at me, and a muscle tensed in his jaw. "I don't care what they say about *me*," he said, almost growling it.

I immediately stood on my toes and kissed his cheek, pleased to see I had the power to make a man blush as much as he did it to me. "Where did you come from?" I whispered, my eyes locked on his and feeling closer to him than I ever had. I didn't know what it was, exactly, but something about this prince made me feel confident. Complete.

A cough broke us apart. "Adam," Gilroy Munroe greeted, and his eyes jumped between the two of us. "Miss Davenport. I'm glad you were able to come. My son was convinced no one would appreciate this as much as you." He held his arm out to the painting on display next to him, and instantly I was captivated.

I'd heard of the painting before, but I'd never seen it in person. Renoir's *By the Water* was breathtaking. Vibrant and soft and soulful. Its two subjects had so much life in them, even though each brushstroke blurred into the next as impressionist works tended to do. Every single corner of the piece had such detail that I could have stared at it for hours, at the way the little boat seemed to rock back and forth and a couple strode by the lake and a breeze caught every leaf.

"Do you like it?" Munroe asked.

It was everything I wished I could paint and knew I never could. "It's incredible," I whispered without looking away from the canvas. "I've never seen anything so…" I just waved my hand, lost for words. Realizing I should probably look at him when I spoke, I turned to the well-named 'King of Art' and bowed my head a little in greeting. "I saw some of your private collection," I admitted with a smile. "Your Seurat is beautiful."

Munroe's face lightened at my comment. Apparently my knowledge of whose paintings he owned met with some approval. "It seems Adam wasn't entirely wrong about you, Miss Davenport. You have fine taste."

I tried not to bristle at his use of 'not entirely.' It was a compliment, even if it contained a hidden insult. "Thank you, sir," I replied.

"I hope you enjoy your evening, Miss Davenport," he said, and with a nod he returned to the rest of his guests.

Adam immediately dropped his arm and intertwined his fingers with mine, drawing my gaze to him. "That was amazing," he said softly. "*You* were amazing."

I did feel some satisfaction, knowing I had successfully had a conversation about art with The King. I never would have thought it could happen, let alone go well. Thank goodness I had spent hours and hours looking at paintings in museums and online in the hopes of finding inspiration for my own work. Otherwise I never could have gotten on Munroe's good side.

And with the way Adam was looking at me, I definitely wanted to be on his father's good side.

"It's every girl's nightmare meeting a guy's parents," I said, a little breathless.

"Well you were perfect," he replied and pulled me closer.

Goodness, how was I supposed to function with a look like that? My heart was ready to pound right out of my chest, my face on fire, and Adam just kept inching closer even though I was sure we had an audience. I was trapped in that gaze, and I knew if I didn't do something I would be hopelessly lost. Or if I *did* do something, I would never make it out the same.

So I quickly glanced out over the small crowd, finding Adam's father to make sure he wasn't watching us.

He wasn't, but his companion was. The dark-haired man next to Munroe looked completely out of place among the well-dressed glitterati, and I realized it was the same man I'd seen at the garden party. And it wasn't just his jeans and black polo that stood out. He looked absolutely uncomfortable, his eyes occasionally darting around the crowd as if he didn't want to be seen.

But inevitably his eyes fell back on us, more specifically me, and when he realized I had seen him, he nodded his head once and turned his attention back to Munroe.

Munroe's demeanor had changed. He spoke quickly, hardly moving his lips, and hunched his shoulders, trying to disappear. I didn't think he was happy to be speaking to the man next to him, and after a moment he jerked his head toward a door and started to head for the hallway. But the other guy grabbed Munroe's arm tight and practically shook him, and suddenly my brother Matthew was there, pulling the pair of them apart and looking angry, an expression I didn't like. Matthew didn't look nearly as angry as the other guy, though, who seemed to snarl as all three of them disappeared through the door, leaving the party behind with hasty backward glances. What was that about?

"Lanna?" Adam asked quietly.

I plastered on a smile, realizing I was probably pulling my eyebrows together in confusion and concern. "Sorry," I said quickly. "I thought I saw someone I knew." I knew how stupid that sounded, considering I knew most of the people in the room, but I stuck with it. "Wasn't him."

"Oh."

"Should we mingle before your father gets after you?" I continued. As much as the intensity between us terrified me, I almost desperately wanted some of it back. At the very least I didn't want Adam to think I didn't want to be there. "I think we can bear a little, don't you?"

Adam's smile was gentle, and he slowly lifted our clasped hands to press my fingers to his soft lips. "Good idea," he said. "If you're with me, I think I can bear anything."

To my complete and utter horror, Adam had barely turned to acknowledge the person nearest where we stood when I realized it was none other than Chandler Wixcomb, my potential suitor who could talk of nothing but horses.

"Chandler," Adam greeted warmly, offering his hand. "It's been a while."

I hadn't seen the guy in several months, and I was delighted to find he still fit the memory I had of him in my head. While he was wealthy to the point of it almost being obscene and therefore should have had ladies swooning over him like Adam did, Chandler Wixcomb didn't quite have the face of a heartthrob. His nose was long on his thin oval face, his eyes farther apart than normal, and his teeth were just a little too pronounced to fit the world's definition of perfect. He was tall and thin, mostly limbs, and his dusty brown hair slipped onto his forehead in a triangle and landed right between his eyebrows.

Someone really should have told the poor man he was spending so much time with his precious horses that he was starting to look like one of them, and I had the sudden urge to paint him with four legs and a tail.

"Munroe," Chandler said. His deep voice always surprised me, because I half expected him to whinny whenever he spoke. "It's nice to see you out and about with your own kind."

Adam's hand tightened a degree around mine, but his expression hadn't changed from his polite smile. "I go where the art is," he said calmly. "The people don't motivate me quite as much. You know Lanna Davenport, right?"

Normally, I would have loved to be anywhere but there and likely would have fumbled over some excuse to run away and disappear. To my immense surprise, I managed an almost real smile and had the sudden realization that I felt pretty much at ease at Adam's side.

Chandler hardly spared me a glance. Apparently he was upset I had never texted him back about his new horse. "You really should come to the races sometime, Munroe," he said, and he seemed to bounce on his feet a bit. Adam, on the other hand, had grown stiffer. "I've got a gorgeous new thoroughbred who has some good odds going for her. You could put that fortune of yours to good work!"

I snorted a laugh that shocked even me. Both men looked at me, and before I could consider the consequences of my words, I explained, "Even I know Adam Munroe isn't stupid enough to gamble."

Though Chandler looked doubtful, Adam grinned at me and bumped his shoulder against mine. "You know that, do you?" he asked and raised an eyebrow.

I narrowed my eyes playfully, and my face burned under The Prince's gaze. "I'm pretty sure I do."

"Have you guys known each other very long?" Chandler asked. He sounded jealous. *Jealous!*

And while I knew I was playing with fire, given my reputation among my peers, I rolled my eyes and was infinitely glad to know my mother wasn't there to see it. "What does it matter to you, Chandler?" I asked and looked at him, though I would have much rather kept looking at Adam.

His face went a little red, but he managed to keep his cool and focus his attention back to Adam. "I could get you an invitation to the Pegasus next year, Munroe. If you're interested."

I didn't know how he did it, but Adam kept his expression warm and directly on me as he replied, which to anyone who actually interacted with people on a daily basis would have been a pretty clear sign that he wasn't very focused on the conversation at hand. "That's a nice offer, but I'll have to pass." This whole mingling thing wasn't working so well, and I wasn't sure Adam remembered that that had been our plan. He just kept his eyes on me, as if there was nothing else he wanted to look at.

"It's the world's richest race," Chandler said, as if that made it more inviting.

Adam's lips twitched in amusement, and he seemed to be asking me a question with those deep blue eyes of his. Whatever it was, I really wanted to say yes. "I don't see the point of dropping a million dollars on a one in twelve chance my horse and jockey cooperate better than the other guys'," he said. His voice had grown softer, which meant I had leaned closer to hear him, and the room had gotten much, much warmer than it had been a moment ago. "If I'm going to gamble anything, my heart has to be in it. And I want to be sure I can win."

He was so close I could smell that citrusy smell that lingered under his cologne. Whatever soap he used, he definitely needed to keep using it. "That's not how gambling works," I whispered.

"Of course it's not," a sharp voice replied.

As if something had grabbed my insides and given them a good squeeze, I suddenly felt sick to my stomach and gripped Adam's hand tighter before I fell over. It wasn't my mother, thank goodness, but Geneva Kennedy wasn't all that much better. She was older, taller, smarter, and a whole lot prettier than me, and I highly doubted she had ever choked on punch or gotten paint in her silky straight auburn hair that was always perfect.

"Lanna," Adam began, but Geneva cut him off.

"Adam, dear, I was really hoping you would tell me about this painting of yours. And you promised last month to give me a tour of your gallery here at the house." She grabbed his arm and literally tugged his hand free of mine so she could take it instead. There was a woman who knew exactly what she wanted, and she was not afraid to fight for it.

Before Adam could even respond to the sudden shift in conversation, he was steered away by a woman who would always be a step ahead of me in every way and was swallowed by the crowd.

"You can't keep this up for very long, Princess," Chandler said behind me.

I tensed. "What?"

His eyes were on the same place mine had been, the spot where Adam had disappeared, but when they slid to me it felt like he was stripping me down until I was nothing but a little goldfish swimming in a pool of sharks. "This game you're playing with Munroe," he said. "Your mom might think she's got this all planned, but everyone can see right through you and your schemes."

"Schemes?" My voice sounded tiny, like it was stuck in my throat. "I'm not playing a game." Except maybe I was. Yes, I liked what little I knew of Adam, but the only reason I was even here was to get both our parents off our backs. If we weren't forced into this world, I didn't think either of us would choose to be here.

Chandler's horsey face twisted into an ugly scowl as he looked me over, as if seeing me for the first time and realizing I was an old, cracked fence.

Coats of paint could only cover some of my many flaws. "Can I give you a bit of advice, Princess?"

Don't call me that, I wanted to growl, but I was too flustered by Chandler's sudden shift in mood to get it out right, so I kept quiet.

Putting his thin hands into his pockets, he glanced around the crowded ballroom then turned back to me. "The whole world is going after The Prince of Art, and he's never going to settle for a girl who doesn't fit into his perfect little world. Save yourself the heartache and give up now, okay?" He clicked his tongue, and then he was gone.

I stood there in the middle of a sea of my peers feeling more out of place than I ever had in my life.

CHAPTER SEVEN

I spent fifteen minutes standing off to the side watching person after person have endless conversations right in front of me. It wasn't like I couldn't start talking to someone, since I knew pretty much everyone there, but it had only taken me a few seconds to realize that the only person I actually wanted to talk to was Adam, and he was nowhere to be found. With anyone else, it would just be small talk and veiled insults, since from my experience the only thing worth talking about among the elite was who was better off. But with Adam there could be more.

But talking to Adam would only work if he was actually here.

It took nearly those fifteen minutes before he found me again, though maybe part of that was because I'd eventually retreated to a corner and found a chair to wait out the rest of the evening. His clothes looked ruffled, his hair slightly mussed on one side, and I had the horrifying feeling that I knew exactly what Geneva had meant by a 'tour of the gallery.' Classic sneak speak for a good ol' makeout session in a deserted hallway.

I sighed at the sight of him coming toward me. I'd really wanted him to be different, but I should have known better. Pretty much anyone who fit into my social circle had rather loose ideas when it came to affection, whether among spouses or partners or even complete strangers. Why would Adam be anything other than the average rich white boy wanting to have a little fun?

"Lanna," he gasped when he caught sight of me. He nearly tripped over someone's foot, which was a little adorable, but his hurried apology didn't delay him reaching me like I would have liked. Really, I should have left the party the minute Adam ran off with Geneva, but I'd been holding out hope. "I'm so sorry."

He didn't look sorry. Not with his face that bright red and a bit of a smile playing at his lips.

"Whatever," I said, hoping I sounded unbothered. I was pretty sure I didn't manage it.

For some reason, Adam glanced over his shoulder and focused on something in the crowd for a second. Then his eyes went wide, and he straightened his shirt with a little cough. I chanced a quick look behind him and saw Matthew on the other side of the room immediately pretending he hadn't just been miming something to him. What was that about? "I didn't mean…" Adam swallowed, rebuttoning his top button before continuing. "I'm going to tell you something that will most likely damage my well-honed and reputed manliness," he said, a little breathlessly.

I stared at him. What was *that* supposed to mean?

Coughing again, he grabbed a nearby chair so he could sit next to me and take my hands. His fingers were surprisingly cold. Given how he'd spent the last several minutes, I would have expected them to be warm. "Geneva Kennedy terrifies me," he said.

Any snarky little responses I had prepared didn't at all work for that. In fact, what he said didn't make much sense in any way. "What?"

His grin was sheepish, and suddenly he was speaking so fast I had to wonder when he'd last said so many words at once. "I tried to take her to the Renoir so I could tell her the facts as quickly as possible and no longer have any obligation to keep talking to her, but next thing I knew she was pulling me out one of the doors and…" He seemed to shrink, pulling his limbs in close as if he would rather disappear than keep talking. "Matthew had to rescue me."

My jaw dropped. Literally. "He what now?"

Shaking his head, Adam looked absolutely mortified. "Like I said. Manly reputation out the window. Geneva scares the hell out of me, and my bodyguard had to pull her off me."

"So…" I was having a hard time not picturing Matthew forcibly grabbing Geneva by the arm and tossing her down the many steps leading from the front doors, but I figured I should probably stay in the moment, especially because Adam was particularly adorable when embarrassed. I had a feeling he was embarrassed a lot more often than anyone knew, but he had found a way to hide it. Maybe he could teach me how to do that trick. "So you didn't…"

"I could try to tell you how much I would have rather been talking about horses with that idiot Wixcomb than spend any time alone with Geneva, but I don't think I could do it justice."

Before my senses caught up to me, I kissed Adam's cheek again and grinned at him. "You poor thing," I said mockingly, and I was delighted to see him smile back when he caught on to my teasing. "It's a good thing you have Matthew then."

Adam nodded with fake seriousness. "He very likely saved my life."

"This is why I try to avoid these things," I replied. "I think you've just given me a good enough reason to never leave the house ever again."

"I hope that's not true," Adam said. And if he hadn't lost his smile so quickly, I might not have believed him.

Oh boy. I'd wanted the intensity back between us, and now I most certainly had it. Now that I did, I wasn't sure it was such a good idea to sit here in a secluded corner with our heads just a few inches apart. "You should probably try that mingling thing before your father thinks you're neglecting your duty as host," I said, and I added a half smile to let him know I wasn't trying to get rid of him. "Clearly I didn't do my job well enough, so I'll just have to step up my game to keep the rest of the crazies off your scent. We can't have you dragged off by any more wolves."

"I'd appreciate that," Adam replied, and when we stood he slipped his arm around my waist and sent a rush of heat through my body. Apparently he was determined to hold onto me this time and not let go.

* * *

We lasted nearly an hour, both of us smiling and chatting and deflecting endless questions about our relationship, which had probably come from our time in the corner, since we hadn't exactly been out of sight. But when Mrs. Foster grabbed my left hand and not so subtly looked for a ring, Adam took me by the arm and led me out of the ballroom for some air.

"Sorry," he said, giving me a pitying smile as he released me. "I knew they'd be curious, but…"

Taking a deep breath, I tried not to focus on his absence. Not easily done when the air around me cooled without his heat, but after an hour of Adam denying we were anything serious, I wasn't convinced our closeness wasn't just for show. I knew that was a ridiculous thought after the many looks he'd given me throughout the evening, but a part of me still feared I was just a tool for him and everything in that room was an act. I couldn't let myself think anything deeper unless I knew, and even then…

I didn't know if I wanted to think anything deeper. Adam may have found Geneva Kennedy frightening, but that was nothing compared to how terrified I was of what I was starting to feel as the evening wore on.

"I think they hit a new level tonight," I agreed. More hesitantly, I added, "What do you think the gossip of the week will be?" Maybe his answer would help me figure him out.

Adam glanced back at the ballroom door, his eyebrows pulled together. He took so long to answer that I almost thought I might have offended him. "They'll think what they want to think," he said, which didn't help me at all. "Should we walk? Some air might do us good." He held out his arm again, but I didn't take it.

I wasn't sure exactly why, since I monumentally enjoyed holding onto him, but I told myself some distance would help me think clearer and just started walking, hoping he wouldn't be too offended and would follow. Luckily, he did.

"So I know you paint," he said as he opened the front door for me. We hadn't really had a chance to talk about each other, which had made the night incredibly confusing. I felt weirdly close to him, but I still knew next to nothing about him, and he definitely knew nothing about me. Apparently he had realized this as much as I had. "What else do you do with your time?"

I laughed once, the sound coming out a little more bitter than I meant it to. "Depends on what my mother has planned," I replied. "I'm not lucky enough to have a job to escape to."

He mumbled something that sounded a lot like, "It's not always an escape." Louder, he asked, "If you did have a job, what would you do?" and jogged slightly ahead of me to open a small gate on the north side of the house.

"I haven't really thought about it before," I replied, a little shocked by my own answer. "Since I knew I wouldn't have the option, it didn't seem like it was worth my time to think about." What *would* I do? I didn't have any skills or business knowledge. Maybe I could be a gardener, though after seeing some of the stuff Javier and his men did to keep the estate up to my mother's standards, I was pretty sure it would take me years to be good enough.

How long has Luke been a gardener? I wondered, and my thoughts strayed to a daffodil in a vase on my bedroom windowsill. Somehow Luke knew exactly how to get under my skin, and I really needed to get it into his head that he couldn't just show up randomly and start making me question my entire life.

"That doesn't seem very fair. Your brother has a job," Adam pointed out, pulling me back to the present conversation.

I had an easy answer for that one: "My brother is a man. Just like I'm supposed to stay at home and be a dutiful wife and mother and raise the kids, he's supposed to go out into the world and make the money. It's the way things are, even if they shouldn't be."

Adam's steps slowed, and he leaned against a stone wall that ran the length of the property. It was too dark to see him well, but somehow I knew he was thinking hard. When he did speak, he was so quiet I barely heard him: "You don't want to be a mother?"

"I didn't say that," I replied, just as soft. "But I mean, you've met mine. She's absolutely insane, and she's not alone. Is that my future? To torment my daughters until they find excuses to be anywhere but where I am? Isn't your mother like that too?"

Something in the air shifted, a chill in the night that pulled me just a little bit closer to Adam as he folded his arms. "My mom died when I was eighteen," he said, and my heart twisted in my chest.

"I'm sorry," I whispered, feeling terrible.

"She was perfect," he replied. "And I don't mean like the women in there.

She was the perfect mom. Tucked me in at night, told me stories, scolded me when I'd done something wrong."

I'd never heard him speak so clearly, so forcefully, and I grabbed the wall for support as I stood there listening to him. Was this the real Adam coming out?

"Not a day went by when she didn't tell me how much she loved me, and she wanted me to have everything in life. Every happiness, every dream. She told me I could have whatever I wanted. Be whatever I wanted. But she taught me that I had to work for it, and if I ever wanted a successful life, I couldn't do it alone." Adam bowed his head, and the air cooled even more.

"How did she die?" I whispered, for some reason desperate to know.

"Cancer," he immediately replied. "They caught it too late to…"

I slipped my hand into his, and he looked up at me with tears shining in his eyes. "She sounds lovely," I told him.

"She was," he said.

I didn't have a clue who this man was. Not really. And I was determined to find out, every little detail until there was nothing more to learn. I had a feeling it would take a long time. *Even better.* "So," I said and tried to lighten the mood with a smile. "If you could do anything, what would you do? What does the great Adam Munroe do with his free time?"

If not for his tears, his smile might have reached his eyes. So close. "I restore cars," he said, suddenly excited. "Well, one car, at least."

"Really?"

He laughed and started pulling me across a cement driveway toward an open garage behind the house. A light was on already, and I could just see the front of a little blue sports car poking out from inside. "You sound surprised," Adam said, and he practically had a skip in his step as we went.

Honestly? "I am," I said. "I never pegged you for a car guy." But there was so much I didn't know about him that I really *shouldn't* have been surprised. Adam could have been big into coin collecting and skydiving for all I knew. "So you've been restoring this all by yourself?"

He shrugged. "No, but my mechanic has been teaching me as we go, so I'm hoping to get better at it and do the next one by myself."

I could see someone bent over the back of the little car, and I guessed that was the mechanic in question. Odd, for him to be working so late on a Tuesday night. "What kind of car is it?" I asked and drew just a little closer to Adam's side. I told myself it was because the night was quickly cooling down, not because I had a nervous churn in my stomach the closer we got. I had no reason to be anxious, especially with Adam next to me.

"A 1961 Ferrari Berlinetta," Adam said with pride. "And last I heard, we've got it so it will 'very nearly run,' as he put it."

"Given a few more tweaks," the mechanic replied and straightened up to greet us.

I *very nearly* fainted.

Luke the gardener gave me a flash of a wink then grabbed a grease-stained cloth as he turned to Adam and said something car-related I neither understood nor cared to. What was he doing there? He chatted with Adam like they were lifelong friends and hardly gave me any more notice than his initial wink, but I had a feeling he knew exactly how I was looking at him. Staring. The rag in his hand was proving useless, unable to remove the black smudging his fingers, but still he absent-mindedly tried to clean them like he'd been doing it for years. He wore just a dirty gray tank top despite the cool night, and his arms—good glory, his arms—were so much stronger than I'd realized. How had I never noticed?

He was a mechanic too? Gardening, painting, cars… Was there anything the man *didn't* do? Though in stark contrast to the much taller prince in a tux, Luke Hawthorne was just as impressive. Just as handsome, only in a more rugged, real sort of way. Adam was kindness and comfort and safety. Just looking at Luke, at his rough hands, I knew he understood the world better than I ever could. He was adventure and fun and life itself.

What sort of cruel twist of fate was this, putting them together in the same room?

"Lanna?" Adam said.

"Hmm?" I blinked, forcing myself to look away from Luke's shoulders. "Sorry, what?"

Furrowing his brow, he studied my face for a moment then said, "This is my mechanic, Luke Hawthorne. Luke, this is Lanna Davenport."

"Ah," Luke said, holding out his hand like he hadn't whisked me away to the most beautiful place on earth the other day. "The Davenport princess. Pleased to meet you."

I could have slapped him, seeing his barely restrained laughter in those impossibly dark eyes of his. But instead I gritted my teeth and grasped his dirty hand as tight as I could. "Hi," I said, leaving it at that.

Then Adam did the worst possible thing and pulled his phone out of his jacket. "Sorry," he said to me quickly. "I have to take this." He slipped out of the garage, his phone to his ear.

Luke started laughing almost immediately, and I searched for something to throw at him. "You should see your face," he said, luckily keeping his voice low. "What, is it so terrible seeing me?"

"What are you doing here?" I whispered back.

He glanced at the car next to us. "Uh. I work here. I thought that was obvious."

"But you work for my father," I argued, trying to understand. I didn't have the energy to deal with this clash of worlds, and Adam was going to come back and for some reason I would have to pretend I didn't know this infuriating man and something was going to go terribly wrong. I just knew it.

Grabbing a tool from a nearby cart, Luke lifted the car's hood and bent over the engine to tighten something. "A guy can have more than one job, you know. Landscaping is great and all, but I've been doing cars a lot longer."

I tried not to look at him as he leaned over the car, but he was hard to resist. Seeing this other side of him, a more intelligent side judging by that complicated engine, was quickly making me realize I knew as much about Luke as I did Adam. Not that I'd spent *tons* of time with the man, but had I really spent all of it talking about myself?

"How's the party?" Luke asked, making me jump. His amused grin brought a blush to my cheeks.

"It's fine," I said.

"How's your prince?"

I glanced behind me to make sure Adam was still pacing the dark lawn and focused on his phone call. "You shouldn't call him that," I said.

"Why not? If you two carry on the way you have been, that's exactly what he'll be."

My stomach did a flip, but before I had the chance to get mad about that comment, Luke spoke again.

"I'm surprised he brought you out here," he said. "His fiancée had no interest in his hobby, so he never even tried showing her the car. Must mean you're something special." That last line came out lower than the others, almost in a growl, and while I very badly wanted to know why he was angry about someone thinking I was special, I grasped onto a different topic I knew I didn't want to approach.

"What happened with her?" I asked. "His fiancée, I mean."

Leaning against the car, he looked over at me and seemed to process my expression before he spoke. "Are we feeling a little jealous?" he asked, narrowing his eyes.

As if. But even as I started to argue, the words caught in my throat. Maybe I didn't know Adam all that well yet, but I knew I liked him more than I should. How could I possibly compete with someone who had gotten far enough to become his fiancée? "That's beside the point," I said as calmly as I could, though I wasn't sure I managed to hide my insecurities.

I was pretty sure I couldn't hide from Luke even if I tried.

Luke straightened up with a grin, tossing the wrench in his hand and catching it after it spun in the air a couple times. Goodness, he needed to stop that before I melted into a puddle where I stood. He had no right looking that good in a tank top when there was a house full of the best-dressed people on the West Coast right over there.

"Well," he said with a small laugh, "it may come as a shock to you, but Adam Munroe is not like your average millionaire."

I was pretty sure I had said the same thing to him only yesterday. "I'm aware," I said.

"And his Miss Dinah Lancaster was exactly like your average millionaire."

Oh. So Adam had broken things off because she was rich? Beautiful? Perfect? Yes, because *that* made sense… Taking a shaky breath, I tried to rationalize Luke's explanation but couldn't grasp any sense of reason. "Why wouldn't he want to marry someone like that?" I asked, though the question came out breathless. *I* was rich. I certainly wasn't perfect, but when my mother had her way I was probably considered beautiful. Was I just one of the masses when it came to the young elites who fell at Adam's feet? Did I scare him like Geneva Kennedy did?

"Relax," Luke said, and he took a step toward me that made me freeze. He was looking at me like… I couldn't even find the words for it, but it made my heart beat a little faster. "You're nothing like those plastic clones up there in that house, which is why he likes you."

My breath caught in my lungs. "He likes me?"

Suddenly Adam's footsteps crunched on the gravel behind me, making me jump. "Sorry," he said, and suddenly I wondered if he knew how to say anything else. "Sometimes work never stops."

"That's why I like cars," Luke answered with a grin. "They can't come crying to you in the middle of the night."

Laughing, Adam held out his hand to me and said, "I hope he didn't say anything terrible, Lanna. He may be one of the best guys I know, but Luke can be a handful, and he doesn't always remember his manners."

Yes he could, and no he didn't. Though I wasn't sure I could call what he said *terrible*. Just illuminating. "He was fine," I said instead of asking Adam to give Luke a good shakedown to make him explain himself, especially when Adam glanced down at his phone one more time and gave the idiot gardener a chance to wink at me again. I glared back and wished I had the power to smack him like I had done to Matthew earlier, but my anger only made Luke choke down a laugh and pretend to drop his wrench so he could duck out of sight.

"Well," Luke said as he straightened back up with his poker face intact, "it has been a pleasure meeting you, Lanna Davenport. I hope I get to see you again sometime."

Adam's hand tightened around mine, so instead of giving Luke a response, I followed the prince out of the garage and back toward the house.

I was pretty sure Luke would give me plenty more chances to get mad at him.

CHAPTER EIGHT

I felt her before I heard her, like I knew she was watching me with those judging eyes of hers. I wished I could pretend to keep sleeping, but she would know. She always knew. Moaning a little, I glanced quickly at the time—6:47am—and told myself it wasn't worth killing her. It would be much easier to swallow the pain of being woken up way too early after staying out until nearly one in the morning.

"Oh good," my mother said and actually grabbed my arm to help me sit up. "You're awake."

I half wondered how long she'd been waiting there, but I decided it was better not to know. "I'm awake," I mumbled back.

"So?"

"So what?"

The flash of anger in her eyes caught me by surprise, and I shrunk away from her as she stood there next to my bed. "What happened last night?"

I went to a party then came home, I wanted to tell her, but I knew she would want details. Usually I had her hovering right behind me, dictating my every move. I was lucky enough she hadn't insisted she go with me to the Munroes' party, so the least I could do was tell her the basic happenings.

"I did everything I was supposed to," I mumbled, and then a yawn interrupted me. "And I was by Adam's side all night, so you don't have to worry." Except when Geneva attacked him, though that wasn't his fault. And for a few minutes when it was just Luke and me in the garage… "I kept to normal conversation topics, and I only rolled my eyes once." Though I was sorely tempted to do it again out in that garage. "Gilroy Munroe and I talked for a minute about art—" and I didn't see him the rest of the night "—and I didn't even trip over my own feet when Adam asked me to dance."

I hoped that would be enough to satisfy her.

She gripped my hand, literal tears in her eyes as she beamed at me. "And you and Adam? Did he…?”

No, he didn't anything. He may have kept me closer throughout the rest of the party, but I was pretty sure that was because all the social interaction was exhausting. For both of us. Without his father there, Adam had had to play host, and the two of us kept each other near to avoid losing the energy we needed to make it through the night. I thought maybe, when he walked me to my car at the end of the night, he might have done something, but there was hesitation in his eyes. I made it easier for him—no girl wants a kiss out of obligation—and gave him a quick hug before slipping into the car.

"No," I said finally. "No, he didn't."

Frowning, my mother seemed to think about that for a good deal of time. Apparently my lack of a kiss or anything was almost as confusing as how she could have ended up with a daughter like me after all the effort she made to produce a duplicate of herself. "We'll just have to try harder then," she muttered to herself and glided away.

I immediately fell back onto my pillows and was instantly asleep.

* * *

To my surprise, I managed to spend most of the day out in the gardens without a single interruption. Every so often I looked up from my canvas and scanned my surroundings, just so I could avoid being startled like usual—I wasn't sure how much my heart could take—but Luke wasn't anywhere in sight. I saw Javier and his other men doing their jobs, but the new recruit had either taken the day off or was actually staying away from me.

I didn't understand why that thought bothered me so much.

Because I was distracted, by the time the sun started sinking and sending long shadows across the estate, my canvas just looked like a mess of paint. I couldn't even really call it abstract art, considering half of it I'd brushed on there just so I would have something for Luke to comment on in case he did show up. But he didn't.

Dinner time rolled around, and even though I wasn't particularly hungry, I knew the cook would kill me if I didn't eat at least something. I had barely touched my lunch, though she'd been telling me stories of culinary school and probably hadn't noticed. Still, Shelly had a tendency to make sure I ate enough after the unfortunate month my mother thought I'd put on too much weight and tried to starve it out of me. The only reason I'd survived was because the young chef snuck me food in between my meals with Mother. So, since Shelly would get concerned if I tried to skip dinner, I begrudgingly headed back inside, leaving my stuff on the porch because I had no intention of keeping the day's painting anyway.

As I walked, I pulled out my phone and finally looked at the couple messages I'd gotten earlier but ignored. Both were from Adam.

Thanks again for coming last night. You were amazing.

Two hours had passed between that and the second one:

I hope you're having a better day than I'm having.

I knew I should respond, probably ask him why his day wasn't great, but for some reason I didn't want to. It wasn't like I didn't like Adam. Quite the opposite, actually. And he definitely made parties like that easier to bear. Maybe it was because he'd gotten a little extra clingy after the garage, and as the day had gone on, I couldn't stop thinking about it. I thought it was because he was tired.

Maybe it was because he was jealous.

Of Luke? It didn't really make sense, but it was the only explanation that fit. It wasn't like Luke had tried anything or even expressed interest, and there was no way my mother would ever let me date someone like him anyway. So Adam didn't have anything to worry about, and the whole idea *didn't make sense*.

Not that I really understood how men's brains worked. His slight over-protectiveness could have been for a different reason entirely or not even existed in the first place.

I ran into my mother halfway to the kitchen and prayed she didn't find something about me she could complain about. I didn't have the energy. But instead of looking me over in search of flaws, she smiled.

"Where are you going?" she asked, sounding almost sweet.

"Dinner," I said. "Where you should be." Had I missed something?

"Oh. Yes, well, I'm not eating tonight."

I stared at her for a moment. That was nothing new, since she was generally concerned about her figure as much as she was about mine, but there was something in the way she said it. Like it was the start to some half-concocted plan that would end with me miserable and hungry. I would have been less concerned if I could hear our chef humming in the kitchen, but the house was silent around us, which meant she probably wasn't here. "Is something wrong with Shelly?" She was my only hope for not starving tonight.

Mother glanced at her watch before she answered, though she did so slowly. It was like she was trying to buy some time. But for what? "I gave Shelly the night off," she said. That alone was shocking enough, but she seemed perfectly thrilled by the idea.

Thank goodness for the internet, though I couldn't be sure the nearest pizza place had ever delivered to the likes of our neighborhood. It could be fun to see the look on the delivery guy's face, but I figured I should be extra sure I needed to risk Mother's wrath if I attempted to get myself a pizza. "What am I supposed to eat for dinner?" I asked carefully, praying the answer wasn't an unapologetic, "Nothing."

The doorbell rang, and she immediately perked up even more than she already was. "I believe that's your dinner right there," she said happily. "Why don't you go get the door?" Get the door? I was about to explain to her that she had taught me since birth that a proper woman never answered her own door when she gave me a little shove and sighed, "Just do what you're told, Lanna!"

Clearly my confusion about Adam and Luke wasn't the end of my suffering for the day. Knowing she didn't like making her requests more than once, I gave in and headed for the front door. Whatever her plan was, it was probably all sorts of complicated and would end up with me trying to eat some weird new health food that was more chemical than actual food, and I would have to sneak down into the kitchen after she went to bed and see what I could find before I wasted away.

But when I opened the door, it felt like every drop of blood drained from my body at the sight of the man on the other side, only to rush back all at once in a blaze of heat.

"Adam!"

His smile was small but warm, his blue eyes deeply apologetic. "Hi, Lanna," he said.

I was going to kill her. Shoving me into every public event was one thing, but Adam didn't deserve being forced on me like this when he probably needed a day off from the masquerades as much as I did. Still, I was happy to see him. Happier than I expected to be, even. "What are you doing here?" I asked, eyeing the brown paper bags he held in his arms. A bouquet of roses poked out of one of them.

"Mr. Munroe!" my mother said sweetly behind me. I refused to look at her. "What a pleasant surprise."

Though he glanced at her, Adam took a slow breath and seemed to be fortifying his resolve. I didn't know what he had to be nervous about, unless he had figured out just how crazy my mother was. "I'm making you dinner," he said finally, ignoring her like I was.

"Ha!" I said before I could hold it back and immediately felt myself pale again. "Sorry, no, I'm not laughing." More than anything I was panicking. I hadn't prepared to spend any time with The Prince of Art today, and I wasn't sure I was emotionally strong enough to handle one on one interaction without a little warning. My heart had jumped into double time, leaving my brain a little too fuzzy to speak like a normal human being. But I knew I had to say something before Adam's slightly hurt expression got any worse. "I just… Making me dinner?" How had my mother come up with this scheme?

More importantly, why had Adam agreed to it?

"Can I come in?" Adam asked, sounding unsure.

"Oh!" I stepped back to let him pass and used the few seconds it took to close the door to gather my thoughts. Adam Munroe was in my house. He was in my house about to…cook me dinner? Seriously? As utterly bewildering as that was, I quickly told myself I likely couldn't avoid the situation, so I might as well try to enjoy it as best I could. Adam, at least, deserved a chance. He was probably forced into this as much as I was.

"You're lucky I didn't have any events tonight," I said. I didn't sound entirely overwhelmed, so that was good.

Adam pinked a little, the bags in his arms crinkling as he held them a little tighter. "Actually," he said, quiet enough that only I would hear, "I made sure of that. I figured your mom probably knew your schedule as well as you did, so I contacted her to find a free night so I could surprise you." Now I was the one who was blushing, but Adam didn't seem to notice. "I hope you're not mad at me, Lanna. I thought we could use some time together that wasn't so under pressure."

"Such a thoughtful boy," Mother chimed in, still hovering at the bottom of the stairs and watching us as if we were the most beautiful sight she'd ever seen.

Say something clever. "I'm not mad," I said and cursed myself for not having been born with my brother Matthew's sense of wit. Surely I could do better than that. "At least not as mad as Shelly will be when she finds out we used her kitchen." I gestured in the direction we should go then led the way. My mother stepped up one stair to get out of our way but didn't disappear like I silently prayed she would.

Adam set his bags on the kitchen counter when he arrived then took a second to take in his surroundings. "Lucky for you," he said, almost under his breath—I had to lean in a little closer to understand him, "I've known Shelly longer than you have."

"No way," I replied. She'd been working for us for years.

Grinning, Adam started pulling ingredients from his bags and laying them out as if he needed to see it all to know where to start. He'd brought several different colors of peppers, some other greens I recognized but couldn't name, a whole bunch of spices, several cheeses, something wrapped in paper that smelled a bit like ham, and an entire carton of eggs. "I met Shelly at a restaurant several years ago," he explained. "The place she worked before she came here. We talked a lot whenever we were both there, and we've been good friends ever since."

"I had no idea," I said. Shelly told me about her culinary school days all the time, like when a guy named Sebastian Horner had bragged about his skills as a chef then gotten all the instructors sick with some undercooked chicken, and she'd talked about her days as a fry cook at some little street corner shack to help pay for school, but she'd never mentioned working at a high-end restaurant. She looked the part, her long dreadlocks always neatly piled on top of her head and her apron clean and wrinkle-free, but I couldn't imagine spunky and talkative Shelly becoming friends with someone like Adam.

"These, uh, these are for you," Adam said, his ears red as he held the roses out to me.

"How sweet!" came a coo from the partially open doorway. She was just out of sight, but I had a feeling Mother had no plans to leave anytime soon. This was going to be a very long night with her hovering over my shoulder.

His jaw clenching, Adam seemed to be realizing the same thing as he stood there staring down at the flowers in his hand. A guy could only handle so much of this nonsense, and he seemed to be reaching his breaking point. And when he left without looking back, as he inevitably would, Mother would probably blame me for it and spend the rest of my life mourning the fact I lost my one and only chance at a proper husband.

Just as I was about to apologize and tell him he didn't have to stay, Adam practically dumped the flowers into my arms but pulled one rose from the bunch. He stepped over to the kitchen door and pushed it open all the way, ignoring the gasp my mother made when she realized she'd been caught (though she recovered impressively quickly and put on a smile). "Thank you for letting me come over tonight, Mrs. Davenport," he said and held the rose out to her. "I think I can take it from here. Have a lovely evening." Then he shut the door with a satisfying click before she even had the chance to respond.

I stared at him. Mother's shadow hovered on the other side of the semi-transparent door for a moment, but to my immense surprise, she moved toward the stairs and disappeared, leaving us alone. And Adam stood there, his shoulders tense and his hands in fists, and I couldn't help but marvel at this man who surprised me more and more with every passing minute I knew him.

"How did you do that?" I asked, unable to keep the amazement and relief out of my voice.

He relaxed as he turned back to me, and his smile warmed the room a little. "I've learned," he said quietly, "that sometimes it takes a firm hand to deal with difficult clients. I had a feeling your mom would be similar."

Cutthroat, my father had called Adam Munroe, but that didn't seem the right word. Compelling, maybe. Persuasive. *Irresistible.* And I grinned at him, because anyone who could get rid of my mother was someone I wanted to keep around. "Thanks," I said, because I felt like I could breathe again. "So what are we making?"

"One of my favorites."

Adam passed me as he returned to the counter, and as he did so he touched his hand to my shoulder. Just a tiny little touch, but it sent a shiver through me, and I sat there in a slight daze as he started searching the kitchen for what he needed. Maybe the night wouldn't be all that bad, especially if Mother had retreated upstairs like I hoped she would. She might come back, but I had no doubt Adam could send her away again, and that made me smile as I sat in my chair at the counter and watched him do his thing.

He had to search a few drawers before he found a cutting board and a small knife. He held them out to me, though I had no idea why. "I'm not saying you have to," he explained, "but would you like to help?"

I'd never cooked a thing in my life. "Only if you want nasty food," I grumbled.

But he smiled, still holding the handle of the knife toward me. "Give it a chance," he suggested. "It's not like you've got anyone to impress."

I took the knife and the cutting board from him, but I didn't move. There was a lot he could mean by that last sentence, and I wanted to figure out his intention. Either he was already so taken with me that it didn't matter if I could chop vegetables, or there was so little chance he even considered a future between us that there was no point in me even trying to win his favor. But which was it? With the way he got rid of Mother, I really hoped it was the first one.

After rummaging through a few more cupboards and finding a large frying pan, Adam turned to me and saw me standing there uselessly. Taking pity, he took the cutting board from my hand and set it on the counter, and then he grabbed the nearest onion and set it on top. "Any size will do," he told me gently. "Just cut it into pieces."

Ah, whatever. Outside of seriously injuring myself, the worst I could do was chop the thing so terribly he realized I was just as hopeless as the world thought, and if he couldn't handle my shortcomings, there was little chance of redeeming myself anyway. Gripping the knife tight, I sliced the onion in half. Almost immediately my eyes stung and watered, and I realized all the onion tear jokes I'd seen on the internet were absolutely true. And for some reason that made me laugh out loud.

Adam paused over a large bowl with an egg in each hand, his eyebrow raised in question.

I gestured at the onion, feeling pretty lame for finding a vegetable so funny. "Onion," I said then wiped a tear with the back of my hand.

He smiled. "I had no idea you had such a tender heart, Lanna."

Without even thinking about how unladylike it was until it was too late, I swung my leg out and kicked him in the shin. "Shut up," I said.

But his smile only grew as he said, "Would it help if I told you the peppers were killed very humanely and died happy deaths?"

Was Adam always this playful? I hoped so. Even as my eyes kept watering, probably ruining my makeup, I felt incredibly at ease standing in Shelly's kitchen chopping onions, and I knew most of that was thanks to the man who cracked several eggs into the bowl next to me and sprinkled in an array of spices that smelled heavenly.

Adam Munroe was the first person who made me feel like I wasn't completely incompetent in all areas of my life, and I had no idea how much I'd needed that until suddenly I had it. Even when he had to teach me how to slice a pepper, something I probably should have known how to do already,

I didn't feel belittled or deficient. After growing up with a mother who constantly focused on my many flaws, it was nice to think I had some good things going for me too.

While Adam joined me in cutting up the rest of the peppers and the other vegetables, he told me about his mother. She, apparently, had been the one who taught him how to cook, and some of his favorite memories were when he was a kid and they would both get up early on Sunday mornings to make omelets. "They were her favorite," he said fondly. He was so light. Loose. He looked more relaxed than I'd ever seen him, a hand towel tossed over his shoulder and an easy expression on his face as he worked and talked without his words sounding forced. Clearly one on one interaction was a lot easier for him than being surrounded by people. No wonder he wanted to spend time away from a social gathering.

As we talked, I noticed his peppers were cut a lot straighter and more uniform than mine, but I tried not to get annoyed by that. I did try a little harder to make mine match his. "What made them her favorite?" I asked, concentrating.

"An omelet can be anything," he said, and it sounded like he was quoting his mother. "You start with your basic mix of eggs, but after that…"

"There's endless possibility," I finished for him as I set my knife onto the cutting board before I cut myself, and it surprised me how tight my chest had suddenly gotten. For me, there was no possibility. Not when my mother had already written the recipe for my omelet. Why did I suddenly feel like I was about to cry? I was thinking about an *omelet* for goodness's sake. My mother would kill me if she knew I was crying in front of her precious Adam, but I couldn't stop myself. And there were no onions to blame this time.

"Lanna?" Adam stepped closer, but he seemed to hesitate. I couldn't blame him, since I had burst into tears so suddenly that I probably looked like an idiot.

Sniffling, I folded my arms around my middle and tried to take a calming breath that only shuddered through me. "Sorry," I muttered. "I feel ridiculous. There's no reason for… Sorry. I'm pathetic, I know."

To my surprise, Adam pulled me into a hug that was both tight and gentle. He didn't seem to mind I was just a ball of mush in his arms, even if he probably had no idea what was wrong with me, and I had never felt so completely safe as I did in his arms. "Never apologize for being you, Lanna," he said quietly. "You can be anything you want to be."

And, thanks to Adam Munroe, for the first time in my life I felt like I had a chance to make my own life, and I couldn't have possibly guessed how freeing that would be.

* * *

I didn't realize I was falling asleep at the kitchen counter until Adam laughed a little and nudged my arm. "Am I boring you?" he asked softly. He'd been telling me about some of the artwork he and his father had sold recently, a topic that normally would have kept my rapt attention if I hadn't stayed up so late the night before.

My face burned, and I sat up straight in my chair to jolt myself awake again. "No," I said quickly. "That's not—"

He wrapped his hand around mine and gave it a little squeeze that didn't help with the whole burning face thing. "Relax, Lanna. I'm only kidding. It's nearly ten."

I glanced at the clock on the microwave and was surprised to see he was right. It hadn't felt like he'd been here for hours. Not at all. Rubbing my eyes, I looked around at our dirty dishes and wondered which of the several silver appliances was the dishwasher. "Shelly won't be happy if we leave a mess," I mumbled, though the thought of trying to clean up made me even more tired than I already was.

Adam found a good way to wake me up a little: he lifted my hand and touched it to his lips, his eyes locked on mine. "You're surprising, Lanna Davenport," he said, though he didn't seem ready to offer up explanation for what that meant. "Shelly told me she'd take care of it."

"But…"

Grabbing his phone, he scrolled to a text and showed me what my chef had sent him: *Don't worry about cleaning up cos I don't trust you with dishes. You know why.*

I blinked a couple times, but my head was still a little fuzzy. "Why wouldn't she trust you with—"

Adam stood, cutting off my question, and offered his hand to me again. "Your mom might not let me come over again if I keep you up too late," he said, and though I knew he was joking, he frowned a little.

I found myself feeling a bit panicked, which successfully brought me back to my full senses. "Come over again?" I asked, and my face seemed to turn even redder than before.

He nodded. "If you'd like me to."

The evening had been one of the best of my life because it was the first time in a long time I hadn't been watching my every move to make sure I didn't do anything disappointing. Even when I'd knocked over my glass of water, Adam had just laughed and grabbed a towel to help me clean it up.

I gave him a little shove toward the door, though my heart wasn't really in it. Pushing him out the door would mean I had to wait to see him until he or my mother found another appropriate activity. If he stayed, I didn't have to be alone. "Time for you to leave then," I said reluctantly. "I'd hate it if Mother didn't let you come again."

His smile was *so close*. It was more genuine than I'd seen yet, but his eyes still seemed unable to join in. What was making it so hard for him to be happy? How could I help him? "Thanks for joining me for dinner," he said as he moved out into the hallway and toward the door, bringing me with him. "I know it can… I hope I didn't invade your personal time."

The house was quiet and dark. Father must have come home at some point, but it looked like he had already gone to bed. I held little hope Mother was already asleep, not with her precious prince inside the house still, but at least she wasn't lurking around trying to spy again. "You're not as exhausting as most people," I said, hoping he knew what I meant by that. Maybe I could clarify. "I like spending time with you."

We reached the front door much too quickly, but Adam paused just before it and turned. He was hard to see in the darkness, but there was just enough light from the kitchen down the hall that I knew he was gazing down at me rather intently. What did he see? Something worth looking at, I hoped. My heart pounded in my chest, and I was pretty sure my hands were shaking, but there was nowhere I wanted to be more than that entryway.

He opened his mouth, closed it, opened it again, and then he closed his eyes, apparently unsure if he wanted to say what was on the tip of his tongue. "Goodnight, Lanna," he said softly, and for half a second I was sure he was going to kiss me. Which absolutely terrified me. But instead he touched his lips to my forehead and lingered there for a moment, and then he was gone, slipping through the door and disappearing into the night.

CHAPTER NINE

Halfway up the stairs to my room, I realized I'd left my paint stuff outside. I was tired enough—and so warm and cozy from Adam's after-dinner goodbye—that I was tempted to just leave it there until morning, but I would never forgive myself if I let any of it get ruined. It had been hard enough to convince my mother to buy the supplies in the first place, and I knew she wouldn't appreciate indulging me for more just because I was neglectful.

So with a sigh, I turned back around and headed out onto the huge back deck where they waited for me.

The night was cool, and the air sent a shock down my spine as if going outside had tugged me back to reality and washed me clean of the evening's bliss. Shivering, I moved to the edge of the deck and looked out over the dark lawn, desperately clinging to my memories of the night. Adam was…surprising. Using his own word, I couldn't believe how much I liked him after only knowing him a few days. He made it so easy to be myself, and I had a feeling that life with Adam would be as simple as the life I had now. How could I possibly complain about that?

My phone buzzed, and I pulled it from my pocket before leaning against the deck's railing. A text from Adam, who hadn't even been gone ten minutes: *I'm glad I met you. Thanks for being who you are.*

I smiled and held the phone to my chest. Simplicity at its finest. "Are you even real?" I whispered out loud, because I was half tempted to believe all of this was just a dream and I would wake up in the morning with Chandler Wixcomb as my best option.

"Not as real as this," Luke said behind me.

I got halfway through a startled curse before I stopped myself, though that didn't keep me from finishing the word in my mind. How could I have possibly forgotten about Luke? I turned to punch him as hard as I could for scaring me but froze when I saw him.

He stood there, the day's painting in his hands and a look of so much concentration that I wasn't even sure if he knew how much he scared me this time around. His expression kept my heart at an uncomfortably fast pace. I'd never seen him this focused, and I hadn't realized anyone could show so much concern. What was he even doing here so late?

He lifted his eyes to me after an immeasurable amount of time, his eyebrows pulled together and a grimace on his lips. "Lanna," he said, so gently and full of emotion that it pulled me closer to him. "Are you okay?"

I'd heard that question so many times in the last few days, but no one had asked it quite like Luke did. Not even Adam, someone who genuinely seemed to understand me. But Luke watched me as the question hung between us, his eyes telling me that until he heard my answer he would think of nothing else.

"I'm fine," I said, knowing he wouldn't believe me even before his face darkened. A moment ago it would have been true, but suddenly I was doubting everything I'd felt during dinner. Adam had never looked at me the way Luke was looking at me right now.

"Lanna," was all he had to say, and his eyes slid back to the painting in his hands. What did he see in that canvas? What had I unintentionally put there? I could barely remember what I'd painted, especially after the distraction at dinner, but apparently there was more to the random splotches of color than I'd realized.

Sighing, I folded my arms and wished I had taken that painting inside before he could find it. Yes, I'd secretly wanted him to come find me in the garden and judge my latest work, but I didn't want him to see everything that he did. I felt far too exposed standing on a dark balcony with my heart on display. "I'm just…" Thinking about Adam. Confused about everything that was happening. Trying to understand my own feelings. And he wasn't helping. "Tired," I said, and he looked up at me again.

"Tired of what?" he whispered.

"All of this." My life wasn't simple. How could I think it was? My life wasn't even my own, and I had no choice in it. Sometimes I didn't even get to choose what I *wore*, and I certainly hadn't chosen to let Adam come over for dinner, no matter how much I enjoyed it. Mother had taken care of that. Was there *anything* I could choose for myself? My whole life I'd felt doomed to be my mother's idea of the perfect omelet, but I had been putting up with that for too long. It was time to start throwing in my own ingredients, to start choosing what I did with my life. The problem was I had no idea how to do that. How did a person start building her own life with her own choices?

The answer stood right in front of me. I had chosen to go with Luke to the observatory. I had chosen to spend hours away from home with him and would never tell my mother about it. "The stars," I said suddenly.

Luke's arm dropped to his side, bringing my painting with it. "What?"

Oh, I was making a huge mistake. But I didn't care. "I want to see the stars, Luke."

I saw the realization spark in his eyes, and then he grinned. Not a smile like Adam's that didn't reach his eyes but a full out grin that made my breath catch in my throat and my heart threaten to beat out of my chest. Luke's smile was real, and I was desperate to cling to it as long as I could.

"Meet me back here in half an hour, Princess," he said and rushed off.

I noticed with a twist in my stomach that he took my painting with him.

I'd never snuck out in my life, so I wasn't completely sure what to do to ensure I didn't get caught. Matthew had done it all the time when we were kids, but I'd never thought to ask him about it, mostly because the idea of breaking rules like that was terrifying. I felt a little silly stuffing pillows under the covers on my bed, but I couldn't rule out the possibility of my mother poking her head in to see if I was getting my beauty sleep. I pulled on my darkest sweatshirt—a gift from Ben after he got his first job and something I kept hidden so my mother couldn't secretly throw the abomination away— and kept my shoes in my hand so I wouldn't make any noise going downstairs.

The thrill of sneaking out brought a smile to my face that I couldn't fight, and I couldn't remember the last time I'd been so excited about something. Not just about seeing real, actual stars instead of the few meager ones we got in the city but about rebelling in such a big way. If my mother ever found out, she would kill me.

I made it to the bottom of the staircase without incident, but then a voice caught my ears and I froze, shoes in hand and my heart racing so fast I could hear it pumping in my ears. But it was just my mother down the hall, talking so quickly into her phone that I could barely understand what she was saying. She *was* awake, just like I'd guessed. But she was several rooms away, so it was my best chance to get away free and clear.

Moving quickly, I toed across the wood floor in my socks and slid around corners, and when I got to the door I opened it so slowly I was sure someone would find me before I could even fit through. But no one did, and I ended up out on the deck without getting caught.

"I'm impressed," Luke said, and even though he kept his voice to a whisper, he still made breathing difficult.

He looked different. Or maybe I was different. But when he smiled and reached his hand out to me, I took it without question.

* * *

We'd made it only five minutes down the road before my head started to spin. I knew I needed to take deep breaths and calm down, but every passing set of headlights hit me with a deeper sense of dread. It was so much worse at night. In the town car after Adam's party, I'd fallen asleep almost immediately, so I missed the whole drive home. But I didn't have the luxury this time, and every inch of me tensed, waiting for something terrible to happen.

"You're okay, Princess," Luke said gently. "I'm not going to let anything happen to you."

I was sure Ben never expected to be hit either.

"Hey. Look at me."

I couldn't. If I looked away from the road, I couldn't be prepared for what might come. What if Ben looked away, and that was why he died? I knew I wasn't the one driving, but that only made things worse. I had no control.

"Lanna." Luke reached over and took my hand, entwining our fingers together, and then he pressed the back of it against his chest. It was faint, but I could feel his steady heartbeat through his t-shirt. "See?" he said quietly. "I'm not scared. You don't have to be either. Have a little faith in people."

I spent the rest of the drive watching him, my hand over his heart and my own beating fast for reasons other than fear. His only communication was through little squeezes of my hand and quick glances my way as he drove, but he said so much in those gestures. Things I wasn't even sure could be translated into words if he tried.

I just wished I understood what they meant.

By the time Luke pulled up outside the old observatory, the anticipation had started making me shiver, though I still hadn't looked away from Luke to see if I could see any stars yet. I just wanted to know what he was trying to tell me, because I had a feeling it was important.

He released my hand slowly so he could turn off the engine, and then he looked at me. His gaze sent a shudder through me, a strange thrill I didn't understand, and then he whispered, "Close your eyes."

I obeyed without question. Here, in the middle of nowhere with only an old building to keep us company, I was free. I could breathe. And I trusted him completely.

He got out of the truck, and a few seconds later my door opened, and he gently took my hands. Helping me down, he led me across the dirt just a few steps. "Climb up here," he instructed, "but don't look up. Please," he added, and he sounded desperate. "Don't look up. Not yet."

He'd filled the bed of his truck with blankets and pillows, and after he boosted me up, I crawled across until I reached the other side. I shut my eyes again to make sure I didn't give into temptation and waited. All sense of exhaustion had left me the moment I stepped out onto the deck, and I sat there in the truck wondering if this was what it felt like to be in control of my own life, to make my own choices and know that no matter what happened next, it was because of me.

Luke's slight cucumber smell filled my nose at the same time I felt his warmth right in front of me. He found my hands again, but not before he pushed a stray lock of hair behind my ear. "Okay," he whispered. "Now you can look."

I opened my eyes, and at first I saw only him. He was so close I could have touched my nose to his if I just leaned forward a little bit. He was watching me, waiting to see my reaction. Then I looked up and gasped.

I'd never seen anything like it. It looked like someone had taken a paintbrush to the sky, or threw up a bucket of glitter on an endless black expanse that stretched beyond what I could see. A stripe of light burst through the center of the sky like a pathway for the gods. So many stars. So many possibilities. It was like the sky spoke directly to me because it knew me. It knew my hopes and dreams, my fears and insecurities, and it was up there telling me not to give up. Everything would be okay because I was so small compared to all of it that happiness wasn't hard to find for someone like me. It was possible. Simply possible.

I wanted to paint it, but I wasn't sure I could ever do it justice.

The heavens above me were so overwhelming that I fell backward onto the pillows, staring upward until I couldn't see through tears. "This is…" I couldn't even find the words. "Luke."

He settled next to me, his shoulder against mine. "Beautiful," he said.

I felt his eyes on me, not the stars, but I couldn't bring myself to look away from the sky to see his expression. But my cheeks burned anyway, the heat spreading through my body. "I had no idea there were so many," I said.

"I tried to count them," Luke replied, almost reverent as he looked up. "When things got bad, and I spent more time here than at home, I spent all night counting them. I figured if I knew how many stars were in the sky, I didn't have to know anything else."

That got me to turn my head. "What was your childhood like?" I knew nothing about this man next to me, and that really bothered me. He, like the rest of the world, knew everything about me, and he was a complete mystery.

Luke met my eyes, a sad smile twisting up the corners of his lips. "I don't think you want to hear about that," he said and pushed some hair out of my face.

No, I really did. Grabbing his hand, I stared at him until he understood.

He took a deep breath, gazing down at our hands. "I didn't really know my father," he started. "He left when I was a kid, and he gave me nothing but a name and a check every month."

He said it like he'd said it many times before, a well-practiced tale of woe. Did he not trust me enough to give me the real stuff? I'd told him about Ben, something I rarely did. Why wouldn't he tell me about his own life?

Luke looked at me, as if he could sense my annoyance. "My mom took that money," he continued, this time looking me in the eye, "and she spent most of it. Usually on drugs. Alcohol. Sometimes I had no idea when I would have food next because we had none. Sometimes I came home from school wondering if we would even have a place to live anymore." He swallowed, and I held his hand tighter. "I found her after school one day," he said, and his voice caught in his throat. "An overdose, and…"

"She was gone," I guessed, and tears filled my eyes again. I blinked them away, refusing to lose sight of Luke.

"We didn't have a phone," he continued, "so I ran until I found someone. They called an ambulance, but I knew it was too late. And Child Protective Services came before the coroner took her away."

"How old were you?" I asked.

He blinked, as if he couldn't remember that far back. "I was eleven," he decided. "But it felt like I'd been on my own my whole life. So when they placed me in a foster home, I didn't know how to handle it. I only lasted a couple years before I decided I just needed to head out on my own. I took to the streets, and I've been by myself ever since."

As lonely as my life could sometimes be, I'd never truly been *alone*. I had both my parents and a brother, and I couldn't imagine not having anyone in my life. Neither could I hold back my tears. "Oh Luke," I said. Could anyone live through a childhood like that and still be so happy? Could anyone live through a childhood like that at all? I had only survived my early years because of my brothers, and without them…

"Don't," he said, reaching up to brush my tears away. "Don't cry over my life."

I couldn't stop. "I had no idea," I wept. "And I keep whining about my perfect life and—"

"Lanna," he said forcefully. "We all have different hardships."

"But I don't," I argued. Compared to his, my life was perfect. "I'm just a sad little princess with everything I could want, and I can't even—"

He suddenly rolled until he was hovering over me on his hands and knees, effectively shutting me up. "Stop," he said, for the first time looking angry. "Lanna Davenport, don't you dare feel sorry for me. I don't regret a single day of my life because it has made me who I am and brought me here, and I won't have you dragging yourself down just because you can't see how your own problems are completely valid. Worry about yourself. I'll be fine."

He was so close. So close, and I couldn't breathe as I stared up at him beneath the stars. What was I supposed to say to that? It wasn't like I could argue when he talked with so much passion behind the words. I had no choice but to believe he spoke the truth. But more importantly, I *wanted* to believe him. I wanted to believe he would be okay.

For a moment, he leaned closer, eyes locked on mine, and my heart pounded in my chest so fast I was sure he could hear it. But then he fell back onto the blankets next to me and let out a sigh. "I stole a broken down car when I was fifteen," he said after a moment of silence. Apparently his history wasn't over. "I took it apart and put it back together until I knew everything about the engine, and then I worked on it, stealing parts from junkyards and using what money I could get to buy oil and gas. Once I got it running, I was able to find work. I learned landscaping and accounting and IT, anything I could read about in the public library."

"Wait," I interrupted, staring at him as we lay there. "You know how to do all of that stuff?"

He grinned, and that smile nearly melted me. "Among other things," he replied. "I don't want to waste my life, since it's the only one I'm going to get. I have big plans for the future."

"So why are you a gardener when you could be doing anything?"

His smile shifted, back to the sad one as he watched me. "Plans don't always work like we want," he said carefully. "But I try to live my life so I'm happy, even if things don't go according to plan. Sometimes that's all we can do. Be happy, no matter our circumstances." So slowly that it was almost like he wasn't moving at all, he reached up and brushed his thumb across my cheek. "Are you happy, Lanna?" he whispered.

I wanted so badly to say yes, and there beneath the stars I felt like I was so close to being able to. But my words stuck in my throat, and more tears pooled in my eyes, and I swallowed the unfamiliar emotion that was building inside me because I didn't know what to do with it.

And instead of answering his question, I said, "Where did you come from, Luke Hawthorne?" It was like he had dropped from the sky to teach me how to live. Straight from the stars.

His hand slid from my cheek, but he smiled again as he shifted slightly farther away from me, though I wished he would come back. I found myself wanting more and more to be close to him. "Same place as all the others, I would guess. Gardening School, obviously."

But though he joked, he brought up another question I was surprised I hadn't asked before. "Actually," I said, "where *did* you come from? My father is extremely picky when it comes to his staff, and he doesn't hire just anyone. You would have had to have a recommendation from someone."

"That's true," he admitted, gazing up at the stars above us.

"And my father rarely trusts anyone who isn't himself," I added.

"I would imagine that's also true."

I shifted onto my side to get a better look at his face so I wouldn't miss anything in his expression. "Who recommended you?"

Now he was definitely avoiding my gaze, his eyes fixed on the side of the truck. "A friend."

Why would he be so cryptic about this? "Luke, what—"

"It was someone who owed me a favor," he said, his voice almost clipped. And since he probably knew I would ask, he quietly added, "I saved his life, so he found me a job when I needed it."

I could tell he didn't want to talk about this, but I couldn't help myself. I was too curious to drop the issue, especially now. "Who was he?" I asked. "And why did he need saving?"

"Lanna." He turned back to me, his gaze harder than I'd ever seen it.

But that didn't stop me. "Please," I begged. I didn't know why, but something told me I had to know who had brought Luke into my life. It was important.

He watched me for a moment, his expression full of concern as he debated his decision, but then he sighed and slowly intertwined his fingers with mine as if that would make it easier to say. "He'd fallen into a dark place before I met him," he said, "and he was alarmingly close to finding an end to it all. I convinced him there was still a lot left to live for."

My stomach twisted, my heart sinking low in my chest. I had my suspicions then, but I was afraid to ask if they were right.

Luke warmed his smile, more than likely aware of my thoughts. "I convinced him he couldn't leave his family behind," he said gently. "Particularly his sister, who had already lost one brother and didn't need to lose the other."

"Matthew," I whispered. Had he really gotten so bad? "You…" My tears were back, but this time there was more joy in them than sorrow. I quickly kissed Luke's cheek, knowing there was nothing I could do to thank him enough for saving my brother. "Thank you," I said anyway. "Why didn't you tell me earlier?" Maybe he wouldn't have annoyed me quite so much, and I could have thanked him sooner.

But Luke looked up at the sky, his expression hard to read in the darkness. "It wasn't really mine to tell," he said softly, "but something like that… Some secrets require trust, and we didn't have that. You didn't know me."

"But you knew me," I replied. He'd acted as if we were best friends right from the beginning, and he'd seen through any flimsy mask I had tried to put up. "Everyone knows me."

"No," he said, and he turned to gaze at me again. There was so much warmth in his eyes that I had to wonder how anyone could dislike this boy who had been through so much. "I had my hunches, maybe. But I know you now. I don't think many people do."

Including myself. I'd spent so long being my mother's daughter that I had no idea who Lanna Davenport even was. "Who am I?" I asked as more tears filled my eyes. If I wasn't Lyra's little princess, Harris Davenport's heir, the most ridiculous girl who pretended to be like the rest of them, who was I?

Luke pushed some hair behind my ear, his hand soft. "You're exactly who you're supposed to be."

"But who is that? I don't know. Tell me." I was almost desperate to know who he thought I was, who I could be if I just knew.

Shaking his head, he smiled and wrapped his fingers around my hand before lifting it to his lips to kiss my knuckles. A shiver passed through me, but it wasn't unpleasant. "You'll figure it out," he told me, "as long as you live life to the fullest. Through the good and the bad, no regrets."

No regrets. I wasn't sure if I was capable of doing that, of being like him, but I wanted to try. I wanted to be happy, no matter the circumstances.

I didn't say much after that. I asked Luke to tell me more about his childhood, about his mother. He told me about his time on the streets and how he learned to take care of himself and others he came across. He told me about when he met Matthew a year earlier and how they quickly became close friends, almost brothers, and Matthew slowly healed after his years of grief until he was back to his old, happy self. And after a while, Luke pointed out a few constellations he knew, and I curled up against him, my head on his shoulder as he traced the stories in the sky.

* * *

I woke feeling more myself than I had in a long time. Not that I really knew who I was, but I felt like I was getting there. Slowly. I'd never had a better night, and I wished I could spend every night learning about Luke Hawthorne and his incredible life. He made the future sound like an opportunity, not an inevitability, and if he could build himself a life from next to nothing, there was hope for me still. Especially if I had him to help me.

But my current life had to catch up to me sometime, and I lay there awake for a long time wishing I didn't have to get back to reality.

I didn't remember falling asleep. I remembered Luke grabbing one of the blankets and pulling it over me, and the night felt like a blur. But waking up in the bed of the truck, with his strong arm wrapped around me and his breath light on my neck, I couldn't help but smile and want to remember every detail of the magical night.

Luke's faint cucumbery scent surrounded me, and I breathed it in deep. Along with it came the freshness of the trees and the crisp scent of chill June air. Summer wasn't fully here yet, and I would have frozen without him there against me. Maybe he knew that, and that was why he curled up close. But I had a feeling it was more than that.

As carefully as I could, I rolled over to face Luke. My movement had to have woken him, but he didn't stir. He looked different when asleep, and I wasn't completely sure why. Something in his worry-free expression, maybe. His hair was more of a mess, falling onto his forehead and into his eyes. Reaching up, I brushed a bit of his hair away so I could see him better.

His resulting smile was breathtaking, sending my heart racing. It wasn't a big smile, not anything close to what I'd seen before, but it conveyed every bit of happiness and contentment I somehow knew he felt. I decided I should paint that smile, so I would never have to let it go. If anything had soul, it was his face in that moment. I wished I could keep that smile forever, and I took in every bit of it, memorizing, until he opened his dark eyes.

"Good morning," he said, barely speaking.

"Good morning," I replied.

"I hope you're not mad at me," he continued. "I was planning on taking you home last night, but you looked so peaceful."

If he had taken me home, I never would have known how comfortable it felt to have his arm draped over my waist. How much I loved looking into his sleepy eyes and seeing nothing but happiness, happiness that I wanted him to have for the rest of his life because he deserved it. He was good and pure and warm, and he deserved the world. I hadn't realized just how much I enjoyed having him around, how much he made the world beautiful, until that moment.

"I'm glad you didn't," I said, and I pushed the rest of his hair from his forehead. "Thank you. For taking me here. For telling me all that stuff. I like learning about you."

He grasped my fingers and gently touched them to his lips, his eyes locked on mine. "Anytime," he whispered.

Suddenly I felt like I had to make a choice, that he was waiting for me to do or say something. He just lay there frozen, his expression fiery and his hands warm and his eyes searching so deep into me that I thought maybe he would find something I didn't even know I had.

And I didn't know what to do.

My phone solved my problem, buzzing somewhere in the blankets beneath me. Jumping, I pulled away from Luke and dug around until I found it between two pillows. How did I suddenly have service up here?

Adam's text stared up at me: *Good morning, Lanna. I hope you slept well.*

Oh boy. Memories of yesterday's dinner suddenly flew back into my mind, and I couldn't believe how easily I had forgotten. What was wrong with me? But even as I stared at the text, my eyes caught sight of the time.

"Oh my—it's 7:30!" I sat up, my heart beating quickly. A few pillows could fool my mother if she looked in, but if she went into my room and woke me up like she had more than once the last week… "Luke, I need to go. Right now."

He stretched out, yawning wide. "Okay," he said, and he sounded thoroughly disappointed. Enough so that if I wasn't slipping into a full blown panic, I might have chosen to stay where I was.

But my mind started showing me visions of my mother's reaction when she realized I wasn't there. What would she do to me? "Oh," I said out loud, "she's going to kill me."

"You'll be fine, Princess."

"Ha!" I dug through the mess of blankets, searching for my shoes. "If— when—she finds out I went out into the middle of nowhere and stayed out all night, she's going to have a heart attack. And not just on my own, which is bad enough, but with you, of all people!"

He sat up quickly, his gaze sharp. "What do you mean, 'me, of all people?'"

Oh come on. I waved my arm lamely. "You know what I meant."

"Because I'm not one of those rich snobs you're parading for?"

Staring at him, I furrowed my brow. Was he really going to do this? I had to go! "That's not what I said."

"Because I'm just a gardener?"

"I didn't—"

Quick and lithe, he grabbed the side of the truck and leapt out, landing easily on the gravel. Without a word, he opened the driver's door and got in, starting the engine a second later.

I climbed out a little less gracefully, nearly falling flat on my face. But I made it into the cab without injury, confused but relieved at the same time. The sooner I got back, the less likely I would lose any semblance of freedom. But Luke was still silent as he revved the engine and pulled back onto the road, much faster than usual, and all hints of a smile were gone. What happened to that vision of contentment he'd given me earlier? Was the memory of it all I would ever get?

"Luke," I said slowly, realizing his knuckles were white on the steering wheel. "Luke, what's—"

"I thought you were different," he said, his voice clipped. Cold. "I thought you could see past all this ridiculous class stuff."

He was upset that I didn't want my mother to know I was with him? But I didn't, because no matter how much I liked him, he did not fit into my mother's painfully perfect world. That would never change. She would look down her nose at him and call him names and treat him like something nasty she'd stepped in. Of course I didn't want her to know about him!

He was driving so fast that I felt like my lungs had stopped working, but I tried to focus, though I couldn't help but grip the door handle as my fear threatened to overwhelm me. "Luke," I begged, my voice weak, "I didn't mean—"

"I know I don't fit into your world," he growled. "I don't need you reminding me of that. But I hoped..." The tires squealed on the road as he made a sharp turn, and my gasp of fear brought his attention to me for a second. Almost immediately he slowed down. "Sorry," he said with a grimace. "I wasn't thinking." I thought maybe that would be the end of the conversation because he barely blinked as he glared at the road ahead, but then he shook his head and sighed. "I'm not mad at you," he said. So who *was* he mad at? With how tensely he gripped the steering wheel, I had a hard time believing it wasn't my fault. I knew I hadn't said things right, but he had to know I didn't mean it like he thought, right?

I didn't know what to say as the silence stretched between us. Even if I tried to explain, I wasn't sure he would listen. He seemed to have forgotten me again, and I sat there in his truck feeling sick to my stomach and altogether miserable as I clung to the handle. How could I make things right?

Luke pulled onto my driveway much too soon, and I still hadn't come up with the right thing to say. He brought his truck around back as much as he could, parking by the other gardeners' cars, and then he was out of the truck before I could even get a word in.

I couldn't end a perfect night like that. I wouldn't. "Luke!" I shouted as I struggled to get out of the car. He was getting too far. "Luke, wait!"

Thankfully he stopped, but he didn't bother turning around. Had I really said something so horrible?

"Will…" I searched my brain desperately. "Will you come back to the deck tonight? I want to show you something." Assuming I wasn't too distressed to paint his smile.

Luke turned his head just enough to see me, and the one eyebrow I could see lifted. "When?" he asked. If nothing else, he was curious.

I knew I risked offending him even more, but it was my only hope: "After dark. So we're not interrupted."

He turned a little more, reading my face, though I had no idea if he liked what he saw. "You should get inside," he said. "We'll talk later." And then he was gone behind our massive shed.

CHAPTER TEN

I barely made it inside the side door of the house and to the stairs when my mother happened upon me, her eyes wide and her posture frantic. *Great,* I thought. *She found the pillows.* But when she saw me, a smile broke across her face and she rushed over.

"Oh good," she said. "You're up. What are you wearing? Nevermind. I just had the most brilliant idea!"

Though confused, I glanced up the stairs. I just wanted a shower. Maybe a nap. At the very least breakfast. I wanted to thank Shelly for letting us use her kitchen, though I wasn't all that hungry after that drive home. "What's this oh-so-brilliant idea?" I asked, knowing I could go nowhere until she told me all about it.

"We're going to have a party!"

I groaned. How many parties would I have to attend before she gave up on me? "When?" I asked. I wanted to know how long I had to prepare myself mentally. And emotionally.

"Tomorrow night!"

Was she serious? I stared at her, waiting for her to laugh at her own terrible joke. My mother was not very spontaneous, and she was even less so when it involved other people seeing her home. Everything had to be perfect, and sometimes she spent months planning even the smallest events. The fact that she'd never mentioned a word of this meant it was a very recent idea.

"Wait," I said. "Tomorrow night? Like, Friday night? No one will even come!" Most likely, everyone on my mother's list would have already had plans.

But Mother still grinned, grabbing my hand and dragging me toward the kitchen. "Nonsense," she said. "People always come if you invite the right ones."

Ah. That only made me worry more. "And, uh, who did you invite?"

"Everyone, of course." She forced me down onto a stool, and within twenty seconds Shelly had a plate of pancakes in front of me and a look that said I had better start eating before she made me eat, though there was also a bit of a glimmer in her dark eyes. I wondered if Adam had told the chef anything about last night, and my heart picked up its pace.

That was not something I needed.

After three bites that mostly just made me queasy, I turned back to my mother. "And who is everyone?" I asked, though I was pretty sure I could name at least two of the guests. Everyone else was just filler, people to make the party seem less like the terrible scheme it was.

"Oh," my mother said as she pulled out her phone and typed away. "Most of the usual people. The Fosters are back in town. Selena Pye, you like her. Oh, and the Munroes, of course."

There it was. "You're just trying to force Adam and me together," I said, scowling. Shelly glared at me from the other side of the kitchen, so I took another bite before she decided to start force feeding me. She had threatened to do so more than once over the years, and she was not someone I wanted to fight against.

"Don't be silly," Mother replied, though she was typing so furiously I wasn't sure she even knew what I said. "Matthew will be here," she added, and a quick glance up at me said a lot. She didn't know Matthew was better. Better thanks to Luke. She thought he was still a hopeless drunk who acted like he had nothing good left in his life.

My stomach twisted, and I turned away from my food to keep myself from throwing up as everything from last night and this morning rushed back into my mind. The good and the bad, and all of it at once was not doing good things to my belly. Or my heart. "Did you know he was working for the Munroes?" I asked my mother.

"Of course I did."

That surprised me. "So you knew he was back in town?"

"Obviously."

"Did you ever go see him?"

Her thumbs stopped, and she looked up at me. For the first time in a long time, she actually looked like a mother who missed her child as she frowned. "How could I?" she said weakly. "He wouldn't even talk to me."

I was angry that it took Matthew so long to let me know he'd gotten out of his depression, but I didn't blame him for not telling *her*. The last time the two of them spoke, she essentially told him to 'suck it up' and refused to believe he had any real reason for acting the way he did.

"You're fine," she'd told him, and that night he had left the house and never come back.

I'd never talked to my mother about Ben's death, and suddenly I wanted to. Had she even cried over her oldest son? I couldn't remember.

"Ben was his best friend," I reminded her. "And he took the loss hard."

My mother swallowed, and for a second I thought I saw a tear or two in her eyes. But then she was back to her no-nonsense self, and she took me by the shoulders and spun me back toward my half-eaten breakfast. "We all took it hard," she said simply. "Now eat up. We have a lot to do to get ready for tomorrow."

* * *

'Getting ready' pretty much involved me sitting in the living room while my mother made phone call after phone call. She instructed me to take notes and check items off the to-do list. While she complained to rental companies and caterers as they probably tried to explain how hard it was to book things on such short notice, I sat there and tried to figure out what I could say to Luke. I probably wasn't going to find any time to paint his smile, but I hoped he would still come meet me on the deck later.

"Lanna? Did you hear what I said?"

I glanced up from the tablet I was staring at and shrugged. "Nope." *I was trying to remember Luke's smile and figure out how to get it back.*

She sighed loudly. "I said the caterer promised shrimp," she said, "so make sure you make note of that. If he doesn't deliver, I'll be sure to charge him for it and make sure he doesn't get booked again. He sounded like he didn't know what he was doing, but he's the only one available."

I typed the info as instructed. Poor caterer. Maybe he was just like Luke and trying to make his way in a difficult world, and he had to deal with people like my mother. I wished there was a way I could help people like that find success without them having to jump through every hoop and go through the trauma of the wealthy's entitlement complex. I wondered if there were others like me who even saw a problem.

The doorbell rang, pulling me out of my thoughts.

"Who...?" My mother leapt to her feet, apparently completely inconvenienced by the interruption. She didn't even wait for someone like the maid to answer the door and went for it herself, something she never did. Either she was starting to forget her own rules, or she was so focused on making this party happen that she wanted to deal with whoever was at the door herself.

That gave me a small break to think of something other than what would be an inevitably terrible party. Unfortunately, all I could think about was having to be stuck in my own house knowing there was a chance Luke was outside. I desperately wanted to talk to him and explain myself, and I had no idea if he would even let me.

Before long, the door to the sitting room opened, and I readied myself for more party planning.

"Lanna?" Adam said from the door.

I jumped to my feet, the tablet in my lap falling to the floor. "Adam!" I gasped. Had I ever texted him back? I couldn't remember. "What are you doing here?"

He had no hint of a smile, and he looked more concerned than I'd seen him. I half expected him to ask me if I was okay, since he seemed to do that a lot, but instead he said, "Can we talk? Maybe outside?"

I could see my mother just behind him, ready to give me the stink eye if necessary. "Of course," I said and followed him out to the deck.

It felt like it'd been weeks since the last time I was with The Prince of Art. Had he really only been here the night before? It wasn't like I didn't want to see him, but I wasn't sure I had the mental capacity to deal with the feelings that were cropping up when it came to Adam. Not on top of everything that was happening with Luke.

Adam walked to the edge of the deck and leaned against the railing, just like I'd done last night. Though I didn't particularly want to delve into anything serious, not after the day I'd had, I joined him and rested my back against the rail.

"Sorry I haven't texted you back," I said before he could say anything. "It hasn't been a very good day." *Though it started off well.*

That brought a tiny smile to his lips, nothing like it should be. "So not much better than mine yesterday."

I hadn't even asked him about his day when he was here last night. What kind of a terrible friend was I? "What was going on?" Did it have something to do with the man I'd seen at the Munroes' house, the one who grabbed Adam's father before Matthew could force them apart?

Adam shrugged. "Work stuff, mainly. It's not important."

I frowned. His answer was so unlike what I could have gotten out of Luke that I felt like it wasn't a real answer at all. And then, as if my thoughts summoned him, Luke came around the corner of the house with a couple other gardeners following behind and a shovel over his shoulder.

"So he does work."

"What?" Adam asked.

My face burned red; I hadn't meant to speak out loud. "I mean, today's been a lot of work."

Luke caught sight of me, and though he gave Adam's back an odd look, at least he offered me a small smile. So I hadn't offended him too badly, at least. That was a relief.

"Getting ready for the party of the century?" Adam asked, amusement in his voice.

"Oh, come on," I said. Mother never ceased to amaze me with her ridiculousness. "Is she really calling it that? It's going to be a disaster at best."

Luke started digging a hole, and I couldn't seem to look away as his arms worked the shovel. There was something methodical about the way he moved. Deliberate. Luke was a man who knew himself, and I envied him for it.

Adam inched a little closer, nudging me with his shoulder and filling my nose with that orangey smell of his that felt like a breath of pure comfort. "I know what can make it better."

I couldn't help but smile. It was almost like I'd forgotten how subtly playful he could be. And how I very much liked that part of him. There really wasn't much I *didn't* like. Adam himself wasn't the problem.

Honestly, what *was* my problem? What reason could I possibly have to not jump into this head first?

I knew exactly what reason, and he was standing several yards away, now watching me while his co-workers fixed a sprinkler.

"As long as you come," I told Adam, trying not to meet Luke's gaze but feeling my face burn anyway, "I'll survive the night."

Adam's grin made my knees weak. Honestly, what was with these boys and their ability to completely make me useless with a single upturn of their lips? It was like I'd never had a guy smile at me before. Maybe I'd never cared before.

Hesitant, I turned around and leaned my elbows on the railing like Adam. "What did you want to talk about?"

I didn't realize men could blush so much, but Adam did it spectacularly. "How about we walk?" he suggested, holding out his arm toward the stables. "I, uh, I wanted to talk about us."

I nearly tripped down the deck stairs, and I noticed Luke snort with laughter as he dug a wider hole. "Us?" I repeated. "But we—"

"Barely met, I know." Adam kept his steps slow, focusing very hard on where he walked and what he said. "Trust me, Lanna. I know it's crazy, and the only reason we even know each other is because of our ridiculous parents. But there's just..." He paused near the stables, apparently unaware of the gardeners working nearby and who would probably overhear us if we weren't careful, and then he turned his full gaze to me and suddenly looked very determined. To do what, I had no idea, which was nothing short of terrifying.

"Lanna," he said, "I think I'm falling in love with you."

I choked, and it took me a few seconds of coughing—and Adam lamely patting my back—before I could breathe again. I heard him wrong. Or this was a weird joke. Or a terrible dream. I'd known this man less than a week! No one could fall in love so fast, especially if they knew it was crazy to do it. It just wasn't possible.

Luke wandered just a little closer, probably to check the other sprinklers but maybe just to torment me. But his expression was wary, almost guarded, and I had no idea what that could mean.

"I'm not expecting you to do anything," Adam continued, "but I figured you should at least know how I feel. When you're around, I don't feel the pressure of my life quite as much, and I can breathe again."

I stood there struggling to find something to say. I couldn't just leave him hanging, not after he told me something absolutely real and personal. But what could I say? "Adam…"

"Just tell me," he said, and I was pretty sure he had rehearsed this whole thing. I could almost see the words pass through his mind before he said them. "Tell me if I even have a shot."

I stared at him. "A shot?"

Nodding, he reached out and took my hand. His fingers were warm, his large hand enveloping mine in a gentle hold that sent a rush of electricity through my skin. "Tell me if there's any chance you could love me too."

Luke's shovel fell from his hand and clattered in the dirt. Adam didn't notice.

I took a deep breath, trying to understand how all of this could have happened so quickly. Did he have a shot? Of course he did. He was kind and considerate, playful and honest. He was everything my mother wanted him to be, which made him a very safe option. He made me feel like I could be myself in this crazy world of ours, and that alone was important. But things had moved so fast.

Luke raised one eyebrow as he watched me, waiting for my response and looking worried.

Swallowing, I tried to give Adam a smile, though I probably just looked sick. "I can see us being very good friends," I admitted, and his face fell. *Wow, that hurts to see.* "And I'm not saying there's not a chance. You're incredible, Adam, and I've never felt as comfortable around someone as I do around you. You don't make me feel like I have to be something I'm not. I just… I can't know anything for sure. I don't think I even know what love is, so how can I predict if I'll feel it?"

Adam nodded once as he pondered that, as if it was some profound answer when really I'd just done my best to avoid the question altogether. "I guess that makes sense," he said quietly, while behind him Luke gave me a warm smile. What was he so happy about? "I know…" Pausing, Adam slowly released my hand, as if he only just realized he still held it. His absence left a surprising gap in my sense of stability, as if holding onto him had made me realize how easily we fit together and how much I needed someone like him to help me stand on my own two feet. "I know that was very forward of me. I shouldn't have… I'll see you tomorrow, Lanna."

As soon as he walked away, it hit me. *I'm falling in love with you.* Adam loved me? *Me?* Of all the people in our world, of all the rich, fancy, proper, *perfect* women he could have picked, he was falling in love with someone like me? I didn't belong in his world. I couldn't even take a drink without spitting it all over someone and her dog, and I had no desire to be a part of the social circle I needed to be. *His* social circle. How could he possibly choose me?

"Breathe, Princess," a gentle voice said behind me. "You handled that like a champ."

Luke's hand at my elbow kept me steady, but it didn't help me breathe any. Nothing made sense. My whole world was crumbling apart, and I had no idea how to hold it together. If things kept going the way they were, I was going to end up freefalling into an unknown I wasn't sure I was ready to face. I just needed something to hold, something to grasp onto until my feet hit the floor again.

"Hey," Luke said, and he gave me a goofy smile as he came around to face me. I knew it was supposed to bring me back to reality, but it just reminded me that he had a much better smile lurking just underneath the surface. A real one. And while he didn't seem angry anymore about what I'd said that morning, I still wanted to try to fix things and get that smile back.

"I'm okay," I mumbled before he could ask if I was.

But Luke shook his head, using his other hand to keep me upright before the ground spun closer. "You don't have to be okay. That was a mean thing he just did. Ballsy, but mean. You've never been in a situation like this, not like he has, and that's a big thing to put on your shoulders without giving you some time to process. I wouldn't blame you for being overwhelmed."

I definitely was overwhelmed. *In love with me.* I'd given up hope that I could ever impress anyone, let alone someone my mother would actually approve of. Was this whole day just a dream? I would give anything to be still asleep in the back of a truck on the side of a mountain, and the first rays of sunshine were about to wake me up and give me the chance to relive this whole day and do it better now that I knew what I was up against.

"Lanna," Luke said, and he drew his eyebrows together in concern.

"What would you do?" I whispered, staring into his face and trying to judge if he'd ever been in love. I wasn't sure I really wanted to know.

He cocked his head, his eyes flicking toward the place Adam had disappeared around the corner of the house. "What would I do?"

Movement at the back door caught my eye. *Mother.* Grabbing Luke, I shoved him through the open stable door and pulled him out of sight before she came to investigate the reason for Adam suddenly showing up. She'd definitely get angry with me for letting him leave so quickly, and I did *not* have the energy to deal with her on top of everything else. I'd handled my max, and I stared at the stable door as it closed next to me, praying she wouldn't suddenly appear there.

I felt his breath on my neck before I realized how close we were. Luke held one hand at my waist, the other on my shoulder, and my hands rested against his warm chest. His heart beat quickly, mirroring mine, and I turned my head until our noses touched.

I swallowed, much too distracted to do anything but continue what I was saying outside. "What would you do if someone asked you if you loved her?"

As he leaned his head back a bit, his eyes jumped between mine, down to my mouth, back up again, and a muscle tensed in his jaw. "What would I do?" he repeated, barely whispering the words as his fingers rose up to caress my cheek. I leaned closer, wishing I understood the fire burning through me, and my movement seemed to give him the push he needed to say what was just on the tip of his tongue. "I'd do this."

When he kissed me, the rest of the world vanished. His lips were soft, gentle, and they searched mine as if they contained secrets. And oh, how I wanted him to know them all. I grasped his neck and pulled him closer, his sweaty, cucumbery scent intoxicating. He took me by the waist as his kiss grew more desperate, deeper and deeper until I was lost in it and I knew nothing but him.

He pulled away much too soon, leaving me breathless and wanting more. Unable to stand on my own, I fell against the wall and pulled him with me, and I felt him smile against my lips.

"I guess that answers that question," he said softly.

I kissed him again, pushing my fingers into his hair as he leaned into me. Our embrace gave me one tiny foothold in my life, one little answer to grasp, and I refused to let it go. At the moment, it was the only thing that made sense.

"Lanna," he said.

I pulled him closer.

"Lanna, I have to get back to——"

"Not yet," I begged. The minute he left, I would have to go back into that house and face the chaos of my life. I just wanted a moment. One moment I could call my own and control.

Laughing, Luke wrapped me into a hug that felt so safe that I didn't want to leave. Ever. "Some of us have jobs, Princess," he said into my neck, making me shiver.

"Do you actually *do* your job?" I asked.

His gentle laugh was the most amazing sound I'd ever heard. "Not when you're around," he admitted, and then he kissed me again, so slowly that I could have sworn time stopped with it.

Mother *would* come looking for me before long. Luke had to get back to work. In the back of my mind I could see Adam's face as he told me he was falling in love with me. But for this moment, everything was good.

I closed my eyes, focusing on the way Luke felt and the way he held me and how blissfully happy I was in that moment. "Come back tonight," I begged him, and then he was gone.

I soaked the last few minutes in, because I had a horrible feeling that things could only get worse from there.

* * *

I couldn't concentrate on anything. If I sat still for too long, like while my mother made more phone calls, I started thinking about what Adam had said to me out by the stables and how I'd given him an awful response. If I snuck away and tried doing something more productive, like working on a painting in my room, all I could see was Luke's face right before he kissed me. It was maddening, and I wasn't sure I could wait long enough for it to get dark to see Luke. I needed something to distract me, and I took to wandering the house after dinner in search of it.

I didn't have to wander far. I caught the sound of Mr. Munroe's name from inside my father's home office as I passed, and I paused in interest because it was an unfamiliar woman who said the name. A moment later I realized Father was watching the news, and the longer I listened the more uneasy I got.

"Munroe was unharmed," the reporter was saying, "but witnesses claim the shooter was clearly targeting the popular art trader, known by locals as the 'King of Art.' No news yet on whether police have been able to track down the assailant, but authorities are urging residents to call the hotline below with any information. In other news, the San Francisco Zoo has…"

My ears seemed to be ringing as I stood there. Someone had shot at Adam's dad? But why hadn't anyone said anything to me? Surely my father could have said something at dinner, unless he was just finding out about this too. When had it even happened? Before or after Adam came over to spring his declaration of love on me?

Darting into the TV room before my father found me lingering outside his office, I fumbled for my phone and typed a hasty text to Adam, though I could barely manage it because my fingers were shaking.

Just saw the news. Are you okay?

He texted back so quickly that he must have been holding his phone already: *I'm fine.*

But that didn't exactly make me feel any better. What if he had been standing next to Mr. Munroe and got shot because of simple proximity? What if Adam was in as much danger as his father?

Are you sure? I asked. *What about your father?*

His reply came fast again: *We're okay. Thanks for checking in.* Was that really all he was going to give me? I was freaking out, and all he could say was thanks? But then my phone buzzed again, this time with a somewhat longer text. *You don't have to worry, Lanna. We have everything taken care of, and this will blow over soon.*

I wanted to believe him, and I mostly did. But I had to know one thing: *Are you still coming tomorrow night?*

As fast as ever, his reply made me smile: *Wouldn't miss it for the world. Goodnight, Lanna.*

Despite his reassurances, I was still on edge, and I slowly made my way back to the sitting room where Mother had been doing her planning. She was talking to a decorator, like she had been before I excused myself to wander, and she didn't seem to notice me sit near her. Weirdly, hearing her irritated voice calmed me down a bit because it was something familiar, unlike seem-ingly random assassination attempts.

Why would someone want to kill an art dealer? Was it the guy I'd seen at the Munroes' parties? Or someone else? Was there a whole crowd of people who didn't like Mr. Munroe's business ethics or taste in art or the prices he offered with buying and selling? There were too many questions, and sitting here wasn't going to help anything.

Before Mother noticed, I slipped out of the room again and went upstairs to my room, grabbing a charcoal pencil and my sketchpad. That, at least, wouldn't remind me of Luke as much as painting did, and I didn't need to add my feelings on that subject to the ones racing through me with Adam.

I scribbled whatever came into my head. Trees, flowers, a bird I had watched from the window earlier that day. And I kept telling myself over and over again that I had to learn to shut my thoughts out or I wouldn't be able to focus on anything. Why was my life suddenly so complicated? If I could just concentrate on one thing at a time, maybe I could function again.

By the time it felt late enough that I could go outside and find Luke, my fingers were aching from holding the pencil and my whole body was tense. I hoped Luke could calm me down like he had in the truck the night before, because I badly needed to relax a bit before I snapped like a rubber band.

"Lanna, where are you going?"

I froze at the back door, my fingers gripping the handle and my heart racing. Mother wasn't supposed to find me. She'd still been in the other room talking to someone on the phone, and I'd hoped that would be enough to keep her busy until I could slip outside onto the deck. It'd been dark for almost half an hour, and I had no intention of keeping Luke waiting any longer. The few hours in between the stable and sundown had been bad enough what with everything going on inside my head and my heart.

Swallowing, I glanced back at her. "I just thought I would get some fresh air."

She narrowed her eyes. Not that I blamed her, since the only time I went outside was to paint, and I had none of my supplies with me. Not to mention it was exceptionally dark out there without the moon to light the yard. "What you need is sleep," she argued. "Just look at those dark circles. Did you even sleep last night?"

I fought the urge to grin. Yes, I'd slept. In the back of a truck with a gardener. *I'm sure she'd love to hear about that.* "I'm fine, Mother. I'll just be out there for a few minutes."

"That's not very safe."

"In my own backyard?" Why was she fighting this so much? Did she know something I didn't? "I'll be—"

"I don't like the idea of you wandering about out there, Lanna." Folding her arms, she settled in a chair that faced the windowed back wall.

I hadn't released the door handle yet, and I stood there trying to figure out how to convince her. It wasn't like I could ask her to come out with me, for so many reasons. "I'm not going to wander," I settled on. "I'll just stay on the deck. Look at the stars." *The few I can see from here, anyway.*

She pondered that idea, and luckily she knew I could be as stubborn as her sometimes. "Fine," she said. "But I'll keep an eye on you from here. Just in case."

That was the best I was going to get, no matter how problematic it would make things. I still had to apologize to Luke for that morning, so I would use the little opportunity I had.

Slipping outside, I tried not to look completely tense as I wandered to the deck's railing. Luckily, Luke wasn't already there, or there would be no way my mother would let me stay outside. I just had to make sure he didn't—

"Hey, Princess."

"Stop!" I hissed, hoping I was quiet enough that my mother couldn't hear through the window. "She's watching."

I saw him out of the corner of my eye, halfway up the stairs and just at the edge of the shadows. "She's watching," he replied, an odd edge to his voice.

"She can't see you, Luke."

All of the air sped out of his lungs at once. "I don't believe this," he growled and turned to leave.

"Luke, wait," I said, hoping he heard every bit of my desperation. "Just listen for a second. That's not what I meant." I glanced over to make sure he hadn't moved, and then I looked out over the yard again before my mother wondered what I was looking at. I had to let go of everything else I was feeling because right now it was Luke who mattered. He was the most important thing. "I know I don't understand," I said after taking a deep breath to clear my head. "What it's like to live a life like yours. I've had everything I could ever want, and I never had to work or save or do anything for myself. I have a chef who makes me whatever I want, whenever I want. I pretend to enjoy charity events when I know they're really just ways to show off and never actually do any good."

I was explaining it all wrong, and out of the corner of my eye I saw Luke fold his arms. "And you," I said, begging myself to make sense of my thoughts. "You actually do good things. You help people, and you create, and you know what it means to earn what you have, and it makes you strong. Valuable. Better."

I turned to look at him. *Let Mother see.* I needed him to know I meant this. "Luke, the difference between you and me isn't money. Or status. Or what we were born into. I would give anything to live your life, because at least you made it your own. Please, Luke. I didn't mean to insult you. I would never hurt you. Believe me. Please." My voice had faltered as I spoke until it was little more than a whisper, and I felt so alone standing there in the lights of the house.

He was too far in the shadows to see his face, but he hadn't moved, and he looked even more tense than before. What had I said wrong? There had to be something I did, and something to make it better. I refused to give up.

"I don't want her to take you away from me," I said. "She won't understand, and I don't…" I swallowed. "Luke?"

His reply was soft, raw, and it sent electricity through me: "Lanna, you have the purest heart I've ever known, and I wish you could see you the way I do. You are so much more than what they want you to be, and… God, I want to kiss you right now."

He wasn't the only one. But I could feel Mother's eyes on my back, and if I had any chance of spending more time with Luke, she couldn't know about him. At all. "I'll find you tomorrow," I told him, wishing tomorrow could come sooner. "I promise."

"I'll hold you to that promise," he said as he stepped backward, and I felt his absence when he left. Like my world was missing just a little bit of its warmth.

CHAPTER ELEVEN

To my surprise, all the preparations for the party went exactly as planned. The house was spotless, the dining room was decked out in all our best china, and the caterer showed up—shrimp included—right on time to join Shelly in the kitchen and get everything ready. Even my hair cooperated, curling exactly how it should. Mother couldn't find a fault with it, though in between making me try on different dresses, she insisted she redo my makeup because I'd apparently never learned how to do it right.

At least the day had gone by quickly and left little room for overthinking. I had done plenty of that last night.

By the time I managed to escape long enough to head to the kitchen for a snack around three—Mother insisted I shouldn't eat lunch, so I would actually have an appetite for dinner and not look completely witless in front of untouched food—I was dying for a chance to go outside and get a least one minute alone with Luke. I'd barely managed to sleep all night because I couldn't stop thinking about our moment in the stable, and being so close to him on the deck without being able to touch him had been more painful than I thought it could be.

I'd also spent the night thinking about what Adam said to me, and that made me more nervous than it should have. What would I say to him? Would he bring up our conversation from yesterday, or would he pretend things were normal and it never happened? I wasn't sure which one I wanted, and just the idea of seeing him again was wreaking havoc on my nerves.

A frantic male voice in the kitchen brought me to a pause just outside, and I peeked in, trying not to be seen.

"You can't do this to me, Jen," the caterer—Josh, I was pretty sure—said into his phone. He had one hand stuffed into his sandy hair, and he leaned against the fridge with wide eyes and a pale face. "Jen. Please. I know it's…

I get that. But this is impo—Jen. Jen. Jen! You can't. I'm begging…" Whoever Jen was, she must have hung up because Josh dropped his hand and stared at the stoves opposite where he stood as if he'd just been given a death sentence.

"Josh," Shelly said suddenly, making me jump. I hadn't seen her over by the pantry. She approached the young caterer with wary eyes, probably recognizing signs of a heart attack like I had. "Josh, what was that about?"

"I'm dead," he moaned, and he tossed his phone onto the counter without caring it could break. "That's it. I'm dead, and I will never find work again."

Shelly put her hand on his shoulder, but her comforting skills usually involved food, not physical touch. She looked as uncomfortable as I felt watching the scene. "What happened?"

"One of my servers is sick," he replied, as if the inconvenience was enough to end the world. "I told her just to work through it, but she said it's contagious, so she can't… What am I going to do? She's gonna fire me, Shelly. I know she is."

Coughing, Shelly pulled her hand back. "That woman is crazy, Josh, but she's not going to—"

"She specifically told me I had to have six servers," Josh interrupted, and his hand went back into his horribly mussed hair. "If I didn't have six, I wasn't worth her time. I had to call in a couple favors to get the last two, and without Jen, I don't have… She's gonna fire me, and this'll ruin me. Do you have any idea what sort of influence the Davenports have?" And then suddenly his eyes locked on me. "Oh my God," he breathed, looking ready to pass out.

Since I'd been discovered, I stepped into the kitchen and met Shelly's eye. I wasn't sure why the caterer would be so terrified of me, and I hoped she could explain.

Luckily, the chef understood my question and put her hand back on Josh's shoulder. "That's just Lanna," she said.

Just Lanna? I wasn't sure how I felt about that.

"You don't have to worry about her," Shelly continued. "She's not like her mother." That, at least, I saw as a compliment.

"You're short a server?" I asked, trying to be as gentle as I could. He thought I was going to tell my mother what I'd overheard and that together we would ruin his short-lived career. Poor caterer.

He didn't have the energy to even nod an answer to my question. He just stood there staring at me, waiting for me to speak his death sentence.

Did everyone see me like that? Shelly obviously knew me better, but I worried the rest of the world thought I was a miniature version of my mother. I looked like her, sure, but that didn't mean I acted anything like her. Especially now. I was my own person, and I needed to figure out a way to prove that to the world.

"Is it a hard job?" I continued.

He furrowed his eyebrows, unable to follow my train of thought. "Not…not really. Carrying a tray around. Drinks and stuff."

It sounded simple enough, and I was sure his other employees could handle the harder things if needed. "So if I found you another server," I said, "you'd be okay? As long as you have six?"

Josh nodded then looked to Shelly, as if he needed her to translate. Shelly just smiled at me, an expression that warmed me to the core.

"I'll be back," I told the caterer. "Don't freak out just yet."

I slipped out of the kitchen, thoughts of a snack forgotten as I searched for the best way to fix Josh's problem. He was right about my mother, and if her every expectation wasn't met, she would do everything in her power to make sure no one hired him again. *Perfection is essential,* after all. All I had to do was find someone capable of holding a tray and keeping silent unless spoken to. How hard could it be?

All I had to do was go right outside and find the one guy I knew wouldn't say no if I asked.

I paused outside the sitting room until I was sure my mother was deep in conversation with whoever was on the other end of the phone, and then I rushed out into the backyard and desperately hoped I had apologized enough that Luke wouldn't take this as an insult. It wasn't because he was a gardener. I was asking him because if anyone knew how it felt to be at the mercy of the rich and powerful, he did.

I just had to find him first.

I passed Javier—he greeted me with a wave as he spoke to a couple of his team—and found a couple gardeners I didn't know by name near the pond, but I didn't see Luke anywhere. "Why is our yard so big?" I mourned out loud, out of breath from my race across the grass. Seriously, the lawn just kept going until it hit the tree line a hundred yards back, and we hardly ever even used it. Ridiculous.

What if Luke wasn't even there? I'd only seen him doing real work a couple of times, and I wasn't sure if he worked every day. But no, he had to be there. I told him I would find him, and he said he would be waiting. He had to be *somewhere* on the estate.

A laugh in the distance pulled me to a stop and sent my heart pounding. Spinning around, I followed a geyser of water down to two people on the far end of the estate where a large stone wall separated our property from the next. *Luke.*

I ran, knowing I wouldn't have long before my mother came looking for me for last-minute party prep. I ran at full speed, straight for the tower of shooting water, and the closer I got the more breathless I became. Luke looked up just before I reached him, and even though he was soaked in muddy water, he was still by far the best-looking part of the garden.

Right as I stopped running, my foot slid in the wet grass and sent me careening forward with a shriek. Naturally, Luke caught me, though my lack of grace nearly pulled him down with me as I grabbed his waist in an effort to balance. Laughter still bright in his eyes, he hoisted me back onto my feet and held my shoulders to keep me steady.

"Careful, Princess," he said, his eyes intense as he gazed at me.

"I don't have a lot of time," I gasped and glanced at the other gardener, who was trying to step on the pipe and keep it from gushing so much water. Instead, he was only managing to spray it everywhere, including on me.

"Go turn off the water," Luke said loudly with a roll of his eyes. "We can't fix a pipe when it's spewing Niagara Falls."

Good glory, he was even more attractive when soaking wet, and the longer I stood there held against him, the more the water soaked into my clothes, but I couldn't seem to find my voice anymore or bother caring about the state of my hair. Not when I suddenly realized we were alone, and all I had to do was lean forward an inch or two and—

Focus, Lanna.

"How do you look in a shirt and tie?" I asked, though it was hard to picture when he was standing there covered in mud.

He raised his eyebrows, completely caught off guard. "What?"

"I… Um…" What was I there for again? I was too trapped in a pair of dark golden eyes to remember. "The caterer," I realized.

That didn't lessen any of his bewilderment, and he pushed me a little farther away to get a better look at my face. "Princess, what—"

"The caterer needs your help," I said. "I mean. I need your help. To help the caterer."

Shaking his head, Luke gently led me away from the geyser, probably because he thought he hadn't heard me right. "I'm very confused," he admitted.

Of course he was. I was bumbling like an idiot because no one had any right to look as kissable as he did just then. I could almost picture the broken sprinkler pipe being a warm summer rain, and if we stood beneath it, it would be just…

The geyser suddenly disappeared, which meant the other guy had gotten the water turned off and would be back soon. I was out of time.

"My mother is crazy," I said in a rush. But he knew that already. "And if everything isn't perfect for her party tonight, she's going to have to blame it on someone. And the caterer is short a server, and I'm trying to find someone to fill in so she doesn't ruin his entire career just because someone got sick and he doesn't have the resources to—"

Luke cut me off with a kiss that was even better than I'd remembered, and heat spread through me even though his hands were icy cold at my neck. "You're incredible," he said against my mouth. "Of course I'll help."

I was too dizzy to reply. How did he do that?

"Hayden's coming back," he said and brushed his mouth against mine.

"Uh huh," I replied, searching for another breathtaking kiss. He tasted just like he smelled. Cucumbers.

"Lanna."

I blinked and shook my head, though Luke's smile didn't help the dizziness. "Right," I mumbled. "I should go. I'll uh…" I took a step back, hoping that would help me think more clearly. It didn't. Not when he was looking at me like that. "Be at the kitchen door by 5:30."

Luke reached out a hand, using his thumb to brush a bit of mud from my cheek. "Anything for you, Princess," he said.

Knowing if I didn't leave soon I wouldn't have the strength to do it at all, I stole one last kiss then stumbled back to the house and through the back door. If I was lucky, I could run upstairs and change before—

"What in heaven's name…" My mother stared at me from the doorway of the sitting room, her phone to her ear but entirely focused on me. "Lanna. How…?"

I decided the truth would be easiest. "I slipped."

Looking on the verge of tears, she lifted her eyes to my head and muttered, "Your hair."

"At least it's not paint," I replied, giving her a sheepish smile. I was way too giddy to be worried by her horror. I had plenty of time to redo it, anyway. "I'll go fix it right now," I added and rushed for the stairs.

Her next comment stopped me in my tracks: "What will Aaron think of you now?"

There must have been something in the air. Or some malfunction of my brain. Whatever it was, I felt anger rising in me and clenching my hands into fists. Turning back to her, I tried to stand taller than her even though we were the same height. "First of all," I said, alarmed by how irritated I sounded, "his name is Adam. If you cared at all you would know that. Second, I don't think he cares what my hair looks like, so I don't know why you try so hard to make me hate everything about myself." I needed to stop. I didn't know what had come over me, but I knew I had to squash it before I said something I regretted. "Third," I said before I could shut myself up, "one day you're going to wake up and realize you can't live through me just because you're too cruel to have anyone actually like you in your own life. I'm not your do over, Mother."

No. Stop. What was I doing? I stood there with wide eyes, waiting for her to erupt. Why did I say that? I'd never lashed out at my mother like that, mostly because I was too scared to see her angry. And now I watched as she stood tense, red rising in her face and her jaw tight.

"Lanna," she said finally.

With that single word I lost all control, and my fear completely overcame me. I collapsed onto the stairs behind me and shut my eyes tight, begging the last few moments to have never happened. Why did it feel like my entire life was falling apart?

"Do you think I like parading you about and spending my every waking moment trying to make up for your deficiencies?" she asked, and every word cut into me. "Do you think I enjoy having a pathetic daughter who cares nothing about propriety and class? Who spends all her days in a fantasy and doesn't realize there's a whole world out there? You have no idea how hard I've worked just to make you presentable let alone desirable, and you think I'm going to throw all that away just because you decided to start acting like a child?"

I could hear her slowly closing in, but I didn't have the strength to open my eyes and look at her face.

"Don't you dare assume you know what I'm doing for you, you ungrateful—"

By some miracle, the front door opened and brought a voice I desperately needed to hear: "Lawn Mower, I'm home! I thought—Lanna?"

I looked up through tears, and Matthew was staring at me as I cowered on the stairs. "Hey," I managed to whisper.

He immediately turned to Mother. "What the hell did you do to her?" he demanded.

She scowled. "Are you accusing me of—"

"Lanna," he tried instead, "what did she say to you?"

Things that were probably too true for me to repeat, so I shrugged.

Matthew took one step toward our mother, and she actually stepped back in fear. I knew he looked different after all his time in the Army, stronger and rougher, but was she really afraid of her own son? "I told you to stop beating her down like this," he growled.

Mother folded her arms, and even though she tried to stand strong, she was breaking fast, her fingers trembling. "I've done nothing of the—"

"I made a promise, you know," Matthew said. "When Ben left."

She flinched at Ben's name but said nothing.

"I promised him I wouldn't let you hurt her," Matthew continued. "Not like you hurt us."

What was he talking about? She didn't hurt any of us. Yes, she was an overbearing mother, but she'd never laid a finger on anyone.

Mother glanced at me, surprisingly pale despite a layer of makeup covering her skin. "Don't be ridiculous," she said, and her voice actually shook. "I haven't hurt—"

"Ben wouldn't have left if you had just listened to him for once," Matthew said, and his voice lost some of its force. "But you decided he had to be a lawyer like Dad, and you refused to hear anything else because him wanting to actually help people didn't fit into your perfect little plan."

I didn't know that part. I stared at my brother, trying to understand. They wanted Ben to be a lawyer? But he was too kind for that. Too gentle. He wouldn't have made it a week as a corporate lawyer like my father.

Matthew stepped forward until he had Mother pinned in a corner, and though I couldn't see his face, I could see her trepidation. As if she knew what was coming. "All these years," he said, and even I shrunk away from the harshness in his voice, "I blamed myself for Ben's death. I convinced him to leave, to rebel against you and go out into the world you tried to keep us away from. So he left, and he had to find a job because he was flat broke after you decided he didn't deserve his inheritance anymore."

Suddenly I was on my feet, staring at my mother as if I'd never seen her before. I thought Ben wanted to be a driver. I thought he was doing it because it would lead him down the right career path or something. He never said he needed the money, so I hadn't even considered…

Matthew wasn't done, and I was pretty sure everything coming out of his mouth was stuff he'd been wanting to say for a long time. "Thank God I got out when I did, but now you're doing it to her," he said, and Mother's eyes flicked over to me again, almost too quickly for me to notice. "Can't you see what you're doing to her? She's twenty-five and barely leaves the house because she thinks she can't go anywhere without a chaperone, so the only time she *does* go anywhere it's one of your ridiculous parties. She thinks painting is a bad thing even though she's crazy good at it and could make a career out of it if she only realized she has serious talent. She can't even sit in a car without having a panic attack because you never let her heal from Ben's death, and you can't even see how hard she tries to fit into a world she doesn't belong."

I couldn't breathe, and I nearly fell back onto the steps as the world started spinning around me. What was he talking about? Was something wrong with me? I didn't… I couldn't…

"I'm not going to let you damage her any more," Matthew said, and his words echoed in my head. "I should have gotten her out of here years ago, but I had no idea it was this bad." Suddenly he was at my side, his hand wrapped securely around mine. "Let's go upstairs," he said and led me up, thankfully staying at my side to help me balance. Otherwise I probably would have passed out on the way to my room.

As soon as he had me settled in my chair, he knelt in front of me and took both my hands. "I'm sorry," he said gently. "That was… I didn't mean to get so mad. But when I walked in and saw you crying, I couldn't just…" He sighed, and he looked like the confrontation with Mother had completely drained him. "She makes me so angry sometimes."

I took a deep breath, and though I couldn't fully comprehend the last several minutes, I did my best. "She tried to make Ben be a lawyer?" I started with.

Matthew nodded, his jaw tight. "Dad said he needed to take over the firm eventually and keep the family name going."

"But he was—"

"Nothing like a lawyer, I know." Frowning a little, he gave my hands a squeeze. "I told him he didn't have to do anything Mom and Dad said because he was his own man."

"You didn't kill him," I said quickly. It wasn't Matthew's fault. I needed him to know that.

My brother smiled, some of the life coming back into him. I'd forgotten how good he looked when he smiled. If he'd stayed in this world, he could have had any girl he wanted. He could probably have any girl he wanted in the real world too, especially now that he was himself again. "I know," he said. "Ben would kill me if he found out I've been blaming myself for this long."

I smiled a little, and Matthew relaxed. I didn't realize how tense he'd been. "Why did Ben think Mother would hurt me?" I asked next. "Why did he make you promise…?"

Sighing, Matthew rose and sat on my bed. "We were only a year apart," he replied, "so Ben and I could keep each other sane. But you were so young and…"

"Naïve," I suggested.

Matthew smiled, shaking his head. "Ben was afraid you wouldn't see the problem with Mom's perfectionism and would just go along with whatever she told you to do, so when he graduated and left home, he made me promise to keep you from falling under her spell. After he died, I couldn't… I couldn't stay here anymore, and I failed you. I'm sorry."

The lingering taste of Luke on my lips said otherwise, and heat rushed into my face as I sat there thinking about what my mother would do if she ever found out about Luke. He certainly didn't fit into her perfect world. "I think I'm okay," I admitted, though Matthew's assessment of me downstairs stung a little, even if he was mostly right. But now that I was safe in my room, away from Mother, I felt like I was forgetting something important. Something that had to do with the gardener. "Oh, I need to tell the caterer he's not losing his job tonight. I found someone to fill in for his missing server."

"Yeah," Matthew muttered, apparently still worried he'd failed our brother as he stared down at the carpet. "Luke is going to make an interesting addition to the night, that's for sure."

I froze. "What?"

Matthew looked up, his eyes wide. "Um."

"That's how you knew I'm afraid of cars," I realized out loud. "Luke told you."

"Um."

Fire blazed in my cheeks as I sat there wondering, "What else did he tell you?" Did he know about the stables? About what happened yesterday?

Matthew blushed too, and suddenly he looked like he wanted to be any-where but there. "He's my best friend, Lanna."

"Oh boy."

"Why do you think I got him the job here?"

I stared at him, so many thoughts swirling around in my brain that I thought I might be sick. This was too much to handle. A person could only survive so much in a week, and I'd hit my limit days ago. "You," I said, even though this wasn't exactly new information. Luke had told me. But... "You got him the job...because of me?"

He shrugged. "I thought you might hit it off. He's one of the best guys I know and the nicest guy on the planet. But then Adam—"

"Oh boy," I repeated. Matthew worked for The Prince of Art. Adam had said he'd heard a lot about me. What, was Matthew trying to set me up with every single guy he knew? "I can't survive this," I groaned. "Tonight's going to kill me, unless Mother does it first."

Matthew grimaced as he watched me spiraling into a ridiculous mess. "Let me worry about Mom, but yeah, I don't envy your evening. I hoped I'd be able to help somehow if I came too. You know, offer emotional support."

Yay. "How much do you know?" I asked. Apparently Luke told him eve-rything as soon as it happened, considering I had only just asked if he would help the caterer. But how much had Adam told him?

Matthew obviously didn't want to have this conversation as he sat there on my bed, his arms folded tight across his chest. Despite how tense he was, he looked at ease in a suit, I realized. Had I seen him wear one since the funeral? I didn't think so. Then again, I'd barely seen him at all since the funeral. "Adam wanted advice," he said. "Before he came to talk to you yes-terday."

I swallowed that, processing slowly. "So you know he's..."

"In love with you, yeah. Or, at least, he thinks he is. That one caught me by surprise."

"Comforting," I muttered. "And Luke?"

"Is in love with you too, obviously."

It felt like my heart stopped dead in my chest, leaving me motionless and dysfunctional in my chair. "I..." I was at a loss for words. How was a girl supposed to react in a conversation like this? "I didn't know that last part," I said as soon as I found my voice.

Matthew paled. "Um. Sorry, Luke."

"He's in love with me?" I whispered, trying to wrap my head around it. Kissing me was one thing. Love was another. Was that why he didn't really answer my question in the stables? *What would you do if someone asked you if you loved her?* Tell your best friend instead of her, apparently.

"Yeah," Matthew said with a little half smile. "Basically since he met you.

Luke never does things by half, and sometimes that gets him into trouble."

So in the course of a week I'd gone from hopelessly pathetic to having two very different men in love with me. And both of them were going to be in the same place all night. *Awesome.* "What am I supposed to do, Matthew?"

Shrugging, he got to his feet and walked over to where Mother had left my dress for the evening. He picked it up and held it out to me, something suspiciously like pity in his eyes. "You deal with the nightmare of tonight, and then you take it one day at a time. You'll figure things out. I know you will. I may have failed you as a brother, but you've turned out alright."

I didn't know how I'd survived so long without my older brother, and tears filled my eyes as I gazed at him. "I'm so glad you're here," I said, and I fell into the hug he offered me. "And you didn't fail."

Someone knocked on the door, and both of us looked up. I had little hope my mother had learned to knock, so I wasn't sure who would be on the other side.

"Lanna?" a soft voice said. "I heard…"

Crossing the room and quickly wiping my eyes dry, I opened the door to find my father standing there. He'd been so busy with a case the last few days that I'd hardly seen him, and it felt strangely good to see someone other than his wife. My father wasn't perfect, but at least he didn't make me feel terrible. Not like she did.

His eyes traveled from me over to Matthew, and he nodded once. "Son," he said, which for him was as good a greeting as he gave anyone.

Matthew nodded back, and he smiled a little. That was a good sign. "Hey, Dad. Sorry it took me so long."

Father's lips tightened, and I wondered what words he held back. Instead, he said, "I thought you would be with Gilroy tonight. Keeping him…" He glanced at me. Why at me? "Safe," he finished, his eyebrows pulling together.

How had I forgotten so completely? Gilroy Munroe had been shot at! And Matthew had probably been there. But before I could ask him if he was and if he was the reason Mr. Munroe had survived, he replied to Father's comment: "He wanted me with Adam while he was out of the house." he said. "Thought it would be…" There was that glance at me again. Did the situation somehow have something to do with me? "Safer."

"Lanna," my father said, "do you mind if I talk to your brother for a bit before dinner? I think… I think we need some time to catch up. Clear the air. Figure some things out."

I desperately wanted to stay and ask more questions, but I didn't want to interrupt this little reunion between father and son, which had its own set of potential problems. I looked to Matthew, and though his grin didn't completely convince me, it told me he'd be fine. If he could stand up to Mother like that, he could handle anything.

"I need to fix my hair anyway," I muttered and retreated into the bathroom with my dress. At least I would be close, in case things went south. If nothing else, I could be a support to my brother like he'd clearly been for me. Even if I didn't know it until now.

CHAPTER TWELVE

Mother and I hardly made eye contact when I went downstairs just before our guests were expected to arrive. Maybe that was because Matthew was directly behind me, but I didn't care about the reason. I was just glad she chose not to comment on my hair or the fact that I'd removed her makeup and done it myself. My father had gone to change a few minutes before Matthew and I headed down, and when he joined us, the doorbell rang for our first attendee.

Mother chose to answer the door herself again—apparently she no longer trusted our maid, Silvia, to do it properly—and I stood with the rest of my family hoping it wasn't Adam who walked through the door into the parlor. I wasn't ready for him. Not yet.

To my relief, Mr. and Mrs. Foster came in with gracious smiles and warm greetings. Mrs. Foster was much like my mother in appearance— tall, thin, and blonde—but she didn't have to try as hard to look flawless. She also absolutely doted on her husband, something I'd never seen my mother do. I couldn't remember a time when I'd ever seen the Fosters apart.

Mrs. Foster, her husband on her arm, came to my father first, thanking him for his hospitality. She greeted me with a fake smile and muttered, "You're looking beautiful, Lanna," though I had a feeling she didn't mean a word of it. *Interesting.* She passed on to Matthew, and her smile widened. "Young Matthew Davenport," she said. "I hear good things about you from Gilroy. Where is he, by the way? I thought for sure we were following behind his car."

At some point Matthew had mastered the fake but polite smile all the rich people wore, and in his tailored suit he suddenly looked remarkably like the rest of the peacocks. Until he opened his mouth: "Oh, Mrs. Foster. Not every Mercedes belongs to Mr. Munroe. You could have been following a rental, for all we know. I'm sure the Munroes will be here soon."

Her perfect skin pinked a little, and she pulled her husband tighter to her arm. "My mistake," she said then touched Mr. Foster's lapel. "I think we should get a drink, dear, until more of our friends arrive."

I watched her cross the room a little more quickly than what would have been natural, and then I elbowed Matthew in the ribs. "What did you do that for?" I asked, though I couldn't keep myself from smiling.

Matthew grinned, rolling his eyes. "She only treated you like that because she was hoping she could get Adam and her niece together. You, darling sister, are the biggest competition in the marriage market at the moment."

Coughing, I stared at him with wide eyes. "Marriage?" I choked. "Do you think Adam wants—"

"Calm down," he replied as the doorbell rang again. "I'm not saying anything like that. But that doesn't mean the ladies don't imagine the worst."

"Because being married to me is so terrible?"

"Because if anyone is good enough for a man like Adam, it's you. And they know it. They don't stand a chance."

"Matthew!" the next guest greeted loudly. Hattie Garcia completely ignored me as she rushed up to speak to my brother, even though we'd been friends in high school. "I hear you've been working with the Munroes. You *have* to tell me all about it."

I needed a drink. Just as I suspected, it seemed people had only accepted my mother's hasty invitation because they thought Gilroy Munroe and his son would be attending. Leaving my family to greet the incoming guests, I followed the Fosters to the other side of the room in search of anything with alcohol. A server stood just behind Mrs. Foster, and I headed straight for his tray of champagne.

"I didn't take you for a drinker," the server said, and I froze with my hand halfway to the tray.

"Luke," I gasped. How had I forgotten already? "You're here."

"You asked me to be."

"I know."

"Are you going to look at me?"

"Nope," I replied immediately. Staring at his chest was bad enough, and I knew if I saw his face, I wouldn't be able to contain myself. He looked so comfortable in a button up shirt and bow tie, and I was afraid to see exactly how well he cleaned up.

Luke shifted the tray to his other hand then leaned closer. "You look incredible," he whispered.

A shiver ran through me, weakening my resolve. After making sure

Mrs. Foster was deep in conversation with Selena Pye, who'd just arrived, I lifted my eyes and met Luke's gaze. Oh boy, that was a bad idea, especially because Matthew's words ran through my head at the same time: *He's in love with you too.* How had I not seen that? Just looking into his eyes I could see it all, and I'd never felt so warm and terrified and overwhelmed in my life.

He really did love me.

Grinning, Luke leaned even closer then whispered, "Breathe, Princess," before stepping forward to offer Selena a glass.

I immediately fell into the nearest chair. I wasn't going to make it through the night. There was no way.

I sat in my chair, completely ignored except for concerned glances from Matthew as people surrounded him with questions and amused smiles from Luke as he moved around the room completely invisible except for his tray, and I didn't feel the need to move until a hush swept over the small crowd. Knowing who had stepped in before I even looked up, I took a deep breath and forced myself to stand.

Adam locked eyes with me almost immediately, a warm smile brightening his face. But it still didn't reach his eyes. Why didn't his smile reach his eyes? There was something in the way, something making it impossible for him to be truly happy. But even as he walked across the room toward me, I wasn't sure I could be the one to help him find that smile. There had to be someone else.

"Lanna," he said when he reached me.

The guests behind him were still silent, waiting for my reaction. Why did they all have to waste so much of their energy on other people's lives? Couldn't they just leave us alone and let us figure all this out without their eyes piercing holes in our backs? I was sick, confused, tired, and I didn't know what I should do. But I did know I had no intention of letting Adam suffer their whispers just because I didn't know how to handle my complicated life. He deserved better than that, especially with everything going on.

So I smiled and let The Prince take my hand. "I'm glad you're here," I said, even if I wasn't sure I meant it. I certainly felt a lot more comfortable now that he was there and I didn't have to endure all the glares on my own. "How was your day?" That sounded ridiculous given what had happened yesterday, so I quickly added, "I mean, how's your dad doing?"

He frowned, but I could tell he was trying to hide it. "He's worried," he said, "but he says it won't be long before they find the guy. I just wish…" He paused and glanced at the crowd behind him out of the corner of his eye. "I'm glad you're with me now," he said a little louder, and then he leaned forward and kissed my cheek, lingering there a moment and letting me breathe in his now familiar smell. "I missed you."

My skin burned where his lips touched, and I found myself replying, "I missed you too." I wished he would be more open about the missing shooter and what he himself was feeling, but Adam must have been even more shy than I thought. After opening himself up to be so vulnerable yesterday, then almost losing his father, he was probably having a hard time dealing with everything, and I probably needed to help him through it. Whether or not he asked me to.

This was going to be a long night. Especially if Mrs. Foster kept scowling at me like that. "Um. Dinner is this way," I said and gestured toward the dining room. "If you're hungry."

"Starved," Adam replied. As we passed my mother, who wouldn't look at me, he paused and said to her, "I'm sorry my dad couldn't make it. He's been, well…"

I looked at my own father, who had retreated to the corner and was deep in conversation on his phone. Just how involved was he with the Munroes' current situation? Mr. Munroe was his client, and maybe they had talked about whoever was threatening him. Was my own father in danger?

"He wishes he could be here," Adam added.

At least Mother looked pleased as she looked down at my arm tucked in Adam's, not that I was trying to make her happy. She beamed as Adam and I continued on toward dinner, and I could only imagine her smugness the rest of the night. I didn't link my arm with Adam's to please her; I did it because neither of us could survive these events without the other. And because after my response yesterday, Adam deserved at least that from me.

"Hey," I said softly, trying to make sure no one who followed overheard. "Will you do me a favor?"

Adam pulled me just the slightest bit closer as he said, "Of course."

"No matter how the food tastes, mention how good it is."

He looked at me, his eyebrows pulled together. He seemed glad of the change of topic, but that didn't make him any less confused. "Uh, okay. Why?"

I could see the caterer Josh peeking out from the kitchen up ahead, and even from a distance he looked sweaty and pale. I really hoped I could help him, and I wondered if there was anyone else out there who cared for the working class. What if I was the only one? "The caterer has worked hard," I said, "and my mother hasn't made it very easy for him. If he fails tonight, she'll make sure no one in our society will hire him."

"And since I'm a Munroe," Adam concluded for me, "my word is as good as gold."

"Exactly."

He kissed my cheek again, smiling at the blush it produced. "I will happily sing his praises. If you think he'll do a good job, I'm sure he will." The fact that he understood my intentions made me immensely warm inside, and I pulled even tighter against his side.

My mother had set up place cards in the dining room, and to no surprise Adam and I were seated right across from each other, though I half expected her to put us side to side. I guessed she wanted the rest of the company to see our 'lovesick glances' or whatever it was people were supposed to do. Once everyone had taken their seats—I noticed Mrs. Foster clear on the other end of the table—Mother tapped her knife against her glass and rose to her feet.

"Thank you all for coming. It's been so long since I've been able to get together with some of you, and you can never go wrong with a good dinner party, isn't that right?" She eyed Adam pointedly, who took a bit too long to realize he was supposed to respond to the rhetorical question.

Coughing, he tried a polite smile and said, "You're very right, Mrs. Davenport. I, for one, can't get enough of these things." And then he gave me a wink.

I barely stopped myself from snorting a laugh. I'd already forgotten—yet again—how much easier Adam made these things. How playful he could be. I never would have guessed I would meet anyone who made this life more bearable, and yet there he sat, his eyes glued to mine. Was the room warm? It felt very warm.

"My thoughts exactly," my mother said. "And now we can eat!"

I think she clapped her hands or something to signal the servers to start bringing in our meal, but I was a little too focused on Adam and the way he kept his foot against mine as if to make sure I knew he wouldn't abandon me to the sharks of the wealthy. Even when the man next to him asked a question, I could practically feel his focus on me. Now how was a girl supposed to eat quail when someone like Adam made her stomach twist in knots?

"A fork is a good place to start," a voice whispered behind me.

I squeaked, quickly praying that those who sat nearest to me were distracted enough by the exquisitely presented food. "Do you have to do this now, Luke?" I hissed back, trying not to move my mouth. I could almost feel him standing behind me where he probably waited with a bottle of wine. I was confused enough as it was, and I wasn't ready to shove my two worlds together. Not now.

"This seems as good a time as any," he replied. "You looked pretty busy a few minutes ago."

"Lanna?" Adam asked, scrunching his eyebrows together. "Is something wrong?"

Eat, dimwit, I told myself and quickly swallowed a bite of roasted potato. "Of course not," I told Adam with a smile. "The food is just amazing, that's all."

He didn't look very convinced as he sat there with his knife and fork in hand. "You look flushed."

"I'm thirsty," I defended.

And then a strong arm reached out from behind and poured me some wine. Luke brushed against my shoulder and sent my heart racing, and for a moment I couldn't do anything but stare at my plate and pray Adam didn't realize why I suddenly couldn't breathe. I had a few words for Luke, none of which I could say with my mother nearby, and I silently begged him to go into another room before I completely fell apart. Asking him to fill in as a server was a terrible idea.

"Lanna?" Adam whispered, and he was already halfway out of his chair and ready to come grab me.

Everyone else had gone silent, watching our exchange with interest, and I could still feel Luke standing behind me, even if he wasn't as close as he'd been a second ago. He did this on purpose, just to see my reaction, and I really wanted to give him that slap he deserved many times before but never got. But if I got face to face with him, there was no way I would be able to resist kissing him. And that would make the night a whole lot more interesting than I was equipped to survive.

I had to pull myself together. Mother was staring at me, Matthew was going back and forth between laughing and worrying, and Mrs. Foster had a ridiculously smug grin on her perfect lips that made my blood boil. She thought I had no chance. That there was no possible way a man as lofty as Adam Munroe, son of the King of Art, would choose someone like me. Just like all the others, she thought I was uncultured and unintelligent and unworthy.

She was dead wrong, and it would take more than this to break me.

Gulping some wine, I took a deep breath and focused on Mrs. Foster, even as she ate her quail as if nothing of interest was happening at all. *Just you wait.* I put on my best smile and channeled my mother as I loudly said, "So Adam, I hear you've been getting a lot of offers on that Renoir your father recently acquired."

Adam dropped back into his chair in surprise, watching me with one eyebrow slightly raised. My sudden change in demeanor had thrown him, but I could see him quickly recovering as he read my expression. A smile played at the corner of his lips as he prepared his own weapons. "We have," he agreed. "Though our appraiser has been giving us a lot of trouble. He's convinced it's a fake. You saw it, Lanna. What did you think?"

I thought it was the most beautiful thing I'd ever seen, and even just a quick glance told me someone would have had to put a lot of effort into forging it. It was possible, but difficult. Extremely. "It's hard to argue against that stroke work," I said.

"Mm," Matthew replied thoughtfully. "The stroke work. Indeed."

I could have laughed, but his overly pompous words had evidently convinced a few of the other guests, who looked back to me with interest. I kept my face as unreadable as I could. "Renoir was much like the other Impressionists, but he still had a distinct style. If someone managed to replicate that, I'd love to meet her."

"Her?" Adam said, and his smile grew. *Almost* to his eyes. "You think the forger is female?"

"You think the painting is a fake?" I returned. "If it is, why couldn't the painter be a woman?"

Adam watched me with such warmth in his expression that it crossed the table and heated me to my core. Goodness, how did anyone keep from blushing when someone looked at them like that? "I guess you'd know better than I would, wouldn't you?" he said. "You are, after all, an expert."

"Expert?" Mrs. Foster choked out suddenly, and I couldn't tell whether she wanted to laugh or bow down and tremble in fear.

"Of course," Adam replied, sitting against the back of his chair and somehow managing to look completely at his leisure at a dinner table. "Didn't you know Miss Davenport is a painter? My dad has already agreed to purchase at least three of her works for his next auction. If we're not careful, Lanna will outshine us all."

My smile dropped along with my stomach, and I stared at Adam. Was that part of our game we'd started playing, or did he really mean…?

The young Prince of Art only smiled more, his elbow resting on the arm of his chair and his eyes fixed on mine. "Munroe Royalties has big plans for Lanna Davenport," he continued softly. "We're hoping she'll be with us for a long time. Exclusively. Unless she chooses to go in a different direction, of course, since she'll have plenty of options."

My control over myself was long gone as I sat there trying to understand. I was pretty sure he was serious, and I couldn't not catch the double meaning in his words. Not that I thought he had any idea about Luke—he hadn't even recognized his mechanic, as far as I knew—but Adam was stating for the entire room, whether they knew it or not, that he fully intended the two of us to be a couple. I just had to make my choice.

Matthew watched me carefully, his eyes jumping behind me to Luke every few seconds. Mother practically glowed with pleasure. My father, even, had his eyes on me, even though he generally occupied himself with his phone or a single conversation and ignored the rest around him. And Mrs. Foster looked like she'd been slapped in the face as she sat open-mouthed and clinging to her husband for support after this shocking revelation.

Not caring those next to us would probably hear, I leaned forward and whispered, "You mean that?" to Adam. "But you've never seen—"

"I don't have to," he replied, even quieter. "I've spent months listening to Matt sing your praises, and now that I know you, I have no doubt you're the sort who puts her heart onto the canvas every time. You can't do that and not have it come out incredible."

A very soft cough in the general area behind my chair brought a wave of sickness over me. If not for Luke, I would have absolutely no idea what it meant to paint my heart. Thanks to him, now I knew.

I had to get out of there.

"Excuse me," I whispered and leapt to my feet before I got too dizzy to stand. My chair tipped backward, but I didn't bother to catch it before I left the room as fast as my feet could carry me.

I only made it halfway to the back door before my knees gave out and sent me sinking to the floor. But a strong hand grabbed my elbow as an arm snaked around my waist and held me up, and I sank into their hold instead of to the floor. His cucumbery scent acted as a sort of refresher, dispelling some of the dizziness. "Luke," I gasped.

"I'm here, Princess," he replied in my ear.

"Lanna!" Adam called. He came up to my other side and practically pulled me away from the man who held me steady. "Lanna, what's wrong? What do…how can…"

"Fresh air," Luke grunted.

I looked up at the gardener, but Adam was already leading me to the door. Luke gave me a smile I didn't have the energy to return, and then he was gone. Luckily, as soon as Adam pushed open the door, the evening air blasted me with a cool breeze that almost immediately soothed the dizziness, though I wouldn't have complained if I only had Luke to fix that problem for me. Adam, however, continued to lead me farther away and helped me sit on a wooden chair looking out over the yard.

"Lanna, you're scaring me," he said before he'd even sat next to me.

Two deep breaths got me nearly back to normal as I rubbed out my temples. "I'm fine," I said. "I promise." And, knowing that wouldn't be enough to convince him, I added, "It's been a long day, and it was just warm in there, is all. And you sorta blindsided me."

Pinking, Adam turned his gaze to the dark, expansive yard and at least looked moderately repentant. "I know. I'm sorry. I was planning to tell you before I left tonight, but Mckenna Foster was acting a little too high and mighty for her own good. I thought maybe it would help things if I said…" A bird or something rustled the leaves of the bushes below the deck, and he looked out into the darkness without finishing his sentence.

"So you meant it." His dad really wanted to sell my paintings? Without even a glance at them? Either he trusted his son's baseless opinion far more than any good businessman should, or there was something more going on. Some piece I was missing. "But you have no idea what I paint. Why would you—"

Grabbing his phone, Adam quickly flipped to something and held it out to me. "That's why," he said, his voice dropping to a rough growl.

I stared at the picture on the screen, unblinking and without breathing. But… It didn't make sense. How would he have…? Adam had a picture of the painting I'd done in the yard two days ago, the one that was just a jumble of colors because I couldn't focus on anything. It looked different now that I understood the emotions behind it. The stripes of dark blue were Adam. The bright splashes of orange and yellow were Luke. And though they very nearly touched in some places, they never once collided as they swirled and circled around a single, tiny tree in the center. Surrounding it but never reaching it.

"Luke," I said out loud. He'd taken the painting after he found it. But did that mean he showed Adam? Why would he…?

Adam sighed. "How long has Luke been working here?"

Looking up from the phone, I tried to judge his emotion based on his expression. But he looked more tired than anything, and I had no idea what that could mean. "About a week," I replied. "I'm not sure." Even though I was. I could think back on the very moment we met with perfect clarity, as if I'd never really left it. Luke was stuck with me whether I wanted him or not.

And I definitely wanted him.

"He showed that to me yesterday," Adam said, waving toward the phone and its picture. "Said if we didn't get you under contract he'd sabotage my car and send me careening off a cliff."

I glanced at the house, but even though it was lit up, I couldn't see Luke. Not even through the dining room windows, where the party was still in full swing. The other servers brought in the next course and were busy doing their jobs, but Luke had gone missing. "Did he really say that?" I asked, though it definitely sounded like something he would say.

Adam chuckled a little and reached for his phone. He grabbed my hand too, effectively pulling my attention back to him. "The guy's too smart for his own good sometimes," he admitted, "and apparently he understands good art when he sees it. I would have bought that painting in a heartbeat without even knowing who the artist was. There's just so much…emotion in it."

"Soul," I suggested, and the word tasted like acid. Not because it was wrong, but because Adam saw the same potential in my art as Luke had, and I was no closer to figuring out what to do about these men who were quickly tearing me in half.

"Lanna," Adam said softly, and his eyes moved to the painting on his phone. "What…what were you painting here?"

Confusion. Loss. Fear. Uncertainty. I didn't have a word that could really describe it. "Me," I settled on. "I was painting me."

His eyes traced the lines of paint, and to my surprise a tear slipped from his eye. "And here I was thinking you'd painted me," he whispered, almost to himself. "This reminds me so much of my mom," he said a little louder. "Back before…you know…"

Before she died. "You miss her, don't you?"

"Of course," he replied, and his hand tightened around mine. "But it's more than that. I miss my life. Back then. Before all of…" He waved his free arm around my large house, as if that explained his thoughts.

It didn't. "What do you mean?" I asked.

"Dad wasn't always rich," he replied immediately.

Caught off guard by the change in topic, I just sat there and waited for him to explain. Most people weren't always rich. My mother had been born into an old money family, but my grandfather on my father's side was the first to make it big when he started his law firm. At least half the families in our circle were fairly new money, so I wasn't sure why Adam's admission was a big deal.

Sensing my confusion, he took a deep breath and dropped his phone on the seat next to him so he could take my other hand and face me. "I mean, Dad doesn't tell people about his past mostly because he doesn't want anyone to realize how…I don't know, how fragile our wealth is? But a decade and a half ago, he was working two part time jobs. I worked as a dishwasher after school every day just so we wouldn't lose the house. So we could eat. So Mom could wear shoes that didn't have holes in the bottom."

I stared at him. The Munroes seemed so comfortable with the elite world that I almost thought this whole thing was a joke. But no, Adam had never been comfortable among the wealthy. And I'd only met his father a couple of times, so how could I say how comfortable he might be? "What happened?" I whispered, ignoring the tears pooling in my eyes. It was like I knew exactly where Adam's little history was going to take us.

Swallowing, Adam shrugged one shoulder. "Mom got sick," he said. "And we knew we couldn't pay for it. We didn't have insurance, and Dad realized that if we wanted any chance of keeping Mom around, he had to work harder so she could get the treatments. Somehow he stumbled across the art trade, and he realized he was good at it. Within months, he was buying and selling pieces worth millions of dollars, and Mom was getting the best care possible."

His mother was gone. Even with the best care possible, she was gone.

"It didn't matter," Adam confirmed, as if he knew my thoughts. "She died anyway, and Dad threw himself into work and became the man everyone knows today. A man focused on appearances and perfection and complication." The tear slid down his cheek, followed by another, and I reached up and wiped them away. Adam leaned into my touch until my palm pressed against his skin. "He forgot what it was like to be normal," he said quietly. "So did I. Until I met you." He leaned closer, his fingers brushing a tear from my own cheek. "You, Lanna, are simplicity."

When he kissed me, I didn't stop him. I welcomed it, even, losing myself in the gentleness of his touch and the pure and raw emotion he put into it. Kissing Adam was easy, like a release from all the convoluted schemes and conniving aunts and overbearing mothers. In a word, it was simple. And when he pulled away and met my gaze, the smile that broke across his face lifted a weight from my shoulders I didn't even know was there.

That smile brightened his face all the way up to his eyes, and for the first time, Adam Munroe looked truly happy.

The gardener standing in the shadows inside the house and trying not to look at us did not.

CHAPTER THIRTEEN

Whether he knowingly did it or not, Adam kept the party going well into the night. He probably just wanted to be the last one to leave, but no one else was willing to miss their chance to be around their precious prince, so conversation carried on and the drinks kept being drunk until even my mother couldn't stop herself from yawning. Mr. Foster had passed out in the corner even though his wife kept chatting with Selena Pye, and Matthew had taken to juggling decorative ceramic balls to keep himself awake.

Around ten, my father had excused himself under the pretense of having important work to do, and he made eye contact with Adam on his way out. Their silent conversation wasn't easy to read, but Adam had grown alarmingly tense until Father was out of the room. Adam only relaxed when I took his hand, but he ignored the question in my eyes and continued his conversation with Davis McCreary. It had to have something to do with the shooter, and it was really starting to bug me that no one would talk to me about it.

At midnight, most of the room had gone silent in a weird stalemate of wills. Who would be the first to crack? Who would decide the endless evening of useless talking needed to end? I certainly wasn't going to do it, and it wasn't just because I worried what that would do to the others' perception of me as someone who couldn't handle this lifestyle. No, I didn't want the evening to end because that would mean Adam would go.

And I really didn't want him to.

I didn't know what it was. Something about sitting at his side, my head on his shoulder and our hands entwined, was so safe and comfortable that I wondered if I'd ever felt so secure in my life. And no matter who we were talking to or how people were looking at us or even if we were in our own little conversation, I could tell something had changed between us. Adam had opened up his past to me. He'd cried, even, and I realized Adam was something completely different from the man the world saw him as.

I couldn't find a better word than the one he'd used: Adam was *simplicity.* Utter, complete, simplicity. When I was around him, I didn't have to pretend to be something I wasn't. I didn't have to worry about what I said or how I acted or who I wanted to be. I could just be me, and I hadn't realized how much I wanted that until he gave me the chance. He made it easy to be a part of my own world as me, something I never would have thought possible. I had always thought I would either have to conform to my world or leave it entirely, but Adam offered a very tempting third option.

I knew I had to deal with the significant elephant in the room, specifically the handsome gardener who had disappeared a few hours earlier along with the rest of the servers, but for now I was content to enjoy the surprising realization that Adam's admission of his feelings wasn't completely unrequited.

"Lanna," Adam whispered, breaking the silence of the room. He kept his voice low enough that it didn't draw anyone's attention, for which I was grateful. I liked it better when it was just the two of us.

"Hmm?" I replied. How easily I could fall asleep right there, without worrying about if I drooled or fell over. I could almost picture him lifting me up into his arms and bringing me up to my bedroom. *Whoa.* Heat blushed my cheeks, waking me up a bit as I forced myself not to get too hasty with my thoughts. *That* had certainly come out of nowhere.

"Lanna, I wanted to thank you."

I thought about sitting up so I could see his face, but I was so comfortable there against his strong arm. It was like I was made specifically to fit right there at his side. "Thank me?" I mumbled. "For what?"

"For being exactly what I need. The world is a whole lot easier to deal with knowing you're in it."

A smile tugged at my lips, and though I closed my eyes, I could picture Adam's face clearly. Particularly the happiness that hadn't left since we were out on the deck. What if I could keep that smile there in his eyes? I certainly wanted to try. "You're not so bad yourself," I murmured back. "I'd never make it through all of this without you."

I felt his lips on my head and immediately snuggled closer to him. "I love you, Lanna," he said. "You know that, right?"

He'd told me twice now, but this time didn't take the air out of my lungs and leave me dizzy. It just settled deep into my chest, next to my heart like a ball of warmth. "I know," I replied. I'd be an idiot not to see it. But I also knew I couldn't just leave his declaration out there hanging in the air between us. He'd given me time, but now I had to make a choice. And whether or not I liked it, that choice was looking pretty easy.

Sitting up, I touched his strong jaw and tried to make sure I said things right. Knowing me, it could go so very wrong. Maybe a kiss first… I leaned in and touched my lips to his, and he responded with a smile so wide it made it almost impossible to do the job properly. But that didn't make it any less worth it, and for a moment I forgot what I was going to say. It was important, I thought, but obviously not important enough if a single kiss could brush it out of my mind.

Oh. Right.

"Adam," I whispered. "I—"

"Well!" Mrs. Foster said loudly, and everyone in the room jumped, either startled out of staring at nothing or jolted awake by the sudden noise. "This has been a lovely evening, hasn't it, dear?"

Mr. Foster grunted, probably too tired to find a proper response.

"I'm very glad you all could come," my mother replied for him with a large grin. She was on her feet, her sudden energy almost impressive. "We'll have to do this again. Soon." And she shot a harsh look at Matthew as he rubbed sleep from his eyes.

"I should be getting Adam back home," he mumbled with a nod, understanding her silent request.

It was the exact thing to get the rest of them up and moving. If The Prince was finally on his way out, they could be too. A low buzz of conversation rose from the silence as everyone got to their feet and tried to wake up enough to make the trip back to their homes.

Adam, however, hadn't moved, and though he glanced at the motion around us, he kept his gaze rather firmly on me. Waiting for me to finish.

"Lanna," my mother said, and her voice settled on me more heavily than I thought it could. I would have thought she'd want to give me time with Adam. After all, it'd been her goal for who knew how long. "Care to help me show our guests out?"

Adam's hand fell from where it had been resting below my ear, and the disappointment in his eyes brought a sharp pain into my chest. I didn't like that expression. At all. With a sigh, he rose to his feet and didn't even offer his hand as he headed for the door.

Ten seconds. Ten more seconds, and I could have said what I needed to say. I didn't know if it would have made things better or worse, but at least I would have said it. Now I wasn't going to get the chance before reality sank back in and made it a hundred times harder. Taking a deep breath, I got to my feet and made to follow Adam before he got too far.

Unfortunately, Matthew stepped into my path with an expression full of worry. "You okay, Lawn Mower?" he asked. "Today has been…"

"A very long day," I admitted quickly. Adam was almost to the door, and I was going to lose my opportunity to be brave and make my own choice for once.

"I just…" My brother sighed, stuffing his hands into his pockets. He looked too much like he had after Ben died, and the fear of him falling back into his depression suddenly rose in me until I could focus on nothing else.

"I want to make sure you're careful."

"Careful?" I repeated.

Nodding, he glanced behind him toward the door. "I don't want you to get hurt. And you're already…"

"Getting torn in half," I finished for him. "I know." Goodness, did I know that part. But I was trying to compartmentalize. Deal with things as they came up, not with everything as a whole. It was the only way I figured I could get through this. "Matthew, what am I supposed to do?"

But my brother simply pulled me into a bone-crushing hug and had no answer.

"I thought you were supposed to be here for me," I grumbled.

"Always," he replied, "but I'm not sure I can help you in this instance. You just have to figure out what you want, Lanna. Preferably before it's too late. I don't want to see either of my friends get hurt any more than I want to watch you suffer."

Well that wasn't helpful at all, and I frowned at him as he put his hands back in his pockets and wandered toward the door. Still, I couldn't let Adam just leave. To my relief, he was standing just inside the door talking quietly to my father, who had apparently come out to say goodnight to his guests. But even though the sight of Adam still there brought warmth back into me, I paused and watched him as he listened to what my father said. He looked…worried. Almost angry.

I'd never seen Adam angry before, and I stared at his expression trying to understand what my father—who rarely spoke unless necessity called for it— could possibly be saying to him. Matthew joined in a second later, with much the same expression on his face. They knew something, and I wanted to know what it was. I didn't want to be left in the dark anymore.

"You should get home," Matthew said quietly and put his hand on Adam's shoulder.

"Wait!" I called a second later and hurried to meet them.

Father acknowledged me with a nod, Matthew said something about waiting outside, and then—thank goodness Mother was out walking Selena Pye to her car—Adam and I were alone.

"Adam," I began, "I know—"

"Lanna." Sighing, he pushed a bit of hair behind my ear. "I'm sorry. I didn't mean to be…"

"I just don't want you to think I…" Wow, neither of us had words for our thoughts.

His terribly blue eyes were tired as they roamed my face, and I didn't think it all had to do with the late hour. Everything that was going on with his company, everything he'd been dealing with all week, had started to take its toll. And still he managed to look at me with those soul-searching eyes as if I was the only thing that could make it better.

"What's happening with your company, Adam?" I asked. If I could, I wanted to help make it easier to bear. "Why would someone go after your father like that?"

Glancing through the open door to where Matthew stood in a tense conversation with my mother, he frowned. "My dad has been having a lot of private meetings with a past client," he said, absently playing with a curl of my hair. "And this man hasn't exactly been courteous." I thought about the man who'd been talking to Munroe at their party earlier that week, the one who seemed to speak daggers and had Munroe completely on edge as they left the party. Was that who Adam was talking about? If it was, and if he was also the shooter, the guy was definitely more than just discourteous. He'd brought a gun into play, and that was terrifying. "Dad hasn't told me much about it or why the guy would attack him like that," Adam continued, "so I hoped yours could enlighten me a bit, since I'm starting to take over Munroe Royalties."

I sensed a 'but' in there. "What's wrong?"

Shoving his hands into his pockets much like Matthew had, Adam looked everywhere but at me. "I'm not sure I know who's in the wrong. I mean, clearly the guy isn't in his right mind, but…"

"You're worried your father isn't being honest?"

"A little, yeah."

That sounded awful. I hated the tension that had stiffened his shoulders over the last few minutes, and I desperately wanted to find some sort of relief I could give him. I had a feeling a kiss wasn't going to do the trick, even though I wasn't opposed to trying. This worry eating away at him was a lot deeper than what I knew how to deal with. "How can I help?" I asked, hating that I had to ask the question at all. If I was a better person, I could have known without needing to wonder. "Adam, what can I do?"

The look he gave me made me weak, and I grabbed his hands to keep myself steady. Good glory, a girl could injure herself with a man looking at her like that. I knew full well I had absolutely no chance at mimicking it, and I silently cursed my inability to express that much emotion in a single half smile. "Lanna," he whispered and pressed my palm to his lips. "You do help. More and more every minute I know you. As long as you're close, I…"

Even if I did tell him I loved him—those three words terrified me—it couldn't possibly compete with what he said. I was out of my element and completely ill equipped to handle this budding relationship of ours. *Relationship*. When had I fallen so hard for him? I had no idea, and I stood there looking up into his face and desperately wishing he didn't have to leave.

As if he knew my thoughts, Adam smiled and quietly suggested, "Walk me to my car."

We walked slowly, passing Matthew and my mother without making any effort to speak to them. I figured Matthew would stay within sight, but I hoped he would keep enough distance to not overhear anything either of us might say. The only thing that stopped Mother from following after us and spying was probably my brother's hand on her arm. I noticed the Fosters' car idling in the driveway still, and yet even knowing Mrs. Foster was likely watching us along with my family, the idea of an audience wasn't as awful as it would have been a week ago.

I didn't care what they thought.

"I'm glad you came tonight," I said softly.

Adam paused at his car without bothering to reach for his keys. He turned to face me, his eyes locked on mine and his hand at my waist. "So am I," he said, his words breathy. He leaned close, his mouth only a few inches from mine. "I'll be anywhere you want me to be, Lanna."

I just wanted him to get a little bit closer, but I couldn't find the strength to close the distance myself. As soon as we kissed, he would leave. "Careful saying that out loud," I said as my heart pounded in my chest. "Mrs. Foster already thinks I have you under some sort of spell."

How could two people be so close without actually touching lips? "She's not wrong," Adam whispered.

"Will I see you tomorrow? I've gotten used to having you around."

His smile was the sort to breathe life back into the world. If I had known how it would feel to see it reach all the way to his eyes like this, I would have tried a whole lot harder. "You can see me any day you want," Adam replied, and then he crossed that speck of space between us and kissed me so deep I couldn't breathe when I came out of it. "I love you, Lanna," he said.

"I love…" I managed back.

Even if I couldn't finish my sentence, Adam grinned a ridiculous grin and seemed to nearly skip around to the other side of his car after he kissed my forehead one more time. Maybe I was wrong. Maybe a kiss really could lift the burden on his shoulders.

Matthew touched my arm as he passed me, and before he could open the car door to get in with Adam, I called out, "Keep him safe, Matt."

My brother smiled, gave me a salute, and then he climbed into the car.

He drives himself, I realized as Adam pulled away, and I watched him go, full of wonder. The Prince of Art, a man people saw as the best of the best, wasn't anything he was supposed to be. He drove his own car—built his own car—and cooked his own food and knew what it meant to have a job and work hard for something. Even though he'd been thrown into a world of wealth and leisure and had every right to sit back and relax, he hadn't forgotten the pains of having nothing. I was sure that for the rest of his life, Adam Munroe would never take for granted the life he had now, and that just made him all the more appealing.

I stood in the driveway long after Adam's car had disappeared, followed quickly by the Fosters. Mother had gone inside and was probably already on her way to bed, likely pleased by my progress with Adam. Not that I cared about her opinion anymore; I could make my own choices, however hard they might be. All the guests were gone, the caterer had long ago left with several new bookings thanks to Adam's praise, and the whole estate sat still and empty.

Almost empty. A single truck sat parked at the side of the house, and I stared at it as my stomach twisted in my gut.

Luke was still here.

Not that I'd forgotten about him, but I had assumed he left with the other catering staff. I certainly hadn't seen him anywhere, and it wasn't like he could do any landscaping in the dark. I had let myself push thoughts of Luke Hawthorne to the side as I focused on Adam—keeping things in neat boxes was easier—but now I stood there and wondered if I should go find him or save that difficult conversation for another day. Halfway to the front door I turned and headed around back for the stables. After that farewell with Adam I was feeling stronger than I had all day, and I knew that determination wouldn't last. If I was going to do this, it had to be now.

I stepped into the dark stables warily. I wasn't sure if Luke was even there, and the trouble with Adam's company suddenly had me a little on edge. Especially if Matthew considered it safer for Adam if he was at home rather than here. If a bodyguard was nervous…

"Aren't you breaking curfew or something?" a soft voice said, making me jump. He sounded so empty, and it was my fault.

I couldn't see him in the darkness, but I looked in the general direction of his voice. "I break a lot of rules when you're involved, Luke."

He laughed once. "Are you saying it's my fault?"

"Yeah," I replied immediately and regretted it. "But I'm not saying it's a bad thing." My eyes had adjusted a little, and a bit of light from the house filtered in through the many windows. I could just barely see him sitting up on top of one of the walls separating the stalls, but I couldn't distinguish his expression. I heard plenty of his emotion in his voice, though, and he wasn't happy. Luke Hawthorne was supposed to always be happy. It was one of the things I loved about him, and it killed me to know he was hurting.

How could I have been so heartless to do this to him? After everything he'd done for me… "Luke, I'm sorry."

"I'm sorry," he repeated, mimicking my inflection and adding a scoffing laugh at the end of it. Did he not realize that he was only making my guilt worse? "You didn't look sorry." So he wasn't sad. He was *mad*. That was even harder to bear.

"Will you come down here so I can talk to you? Please?"

Even if I couldn't see him, I could have sworn he rolled his eyes. "If my princess commands," he grumbled and dropped to the ground. I used the time it took him to step through the stall door and come stand in front of me to try to figure out what I might say, but then he bowed low and added, "What can I do for you, my liege?"

My blood boiled with annoyance. This wasn't my fault! "Don't start that," I growled.

He smirked, still in his bow. "Isn't this how servants should act?"

"You're not a—"

"Or would you rather I get down on my knees?" He did so, his eyes hard as he looked up at me. "This is where I belong, isn't it?"

That was what this was about? Seriously? "Don't be an idiot," I snapped. "You know I don't think—"

"Shouldn't you be off parading about with your handsome prince somewhere?" Luke said as he got back to his feet. "After all, he's at your level like he should be. He won't drag you down."

Folding my arms, I glared at him. "Will you stop? This doesn't have to be about Adam."

"The hell it doesn't."

"You don't have to be jealous."

"Jealous?" He spat the word and moved for the door. "It's not like I have any right to tell you who to kiss."

"Luke."

"And Adam's a great guy. He really is. You'd be stupid not to—"

"Luke!"

"What do you want me to say?" he asked, spinning around to face me. "That I'm an idiot for thinking I had a chance even when I knew the perfect prince was in love with you? Because I don't need you to point that out. I know I'm way beneath you. You want me to say I'm happy for you because you found someone your mother won't look at like something that came out of the trash? You want me to sit back and smile and tell you it doesn't matter what you do as long as you're happy?" His voice broke, and with it so did his body. He fell against a stall door and slid to the ground, staring at the opposite door with a pained expression.

"Of course I want you to be happy," he said, "but I can't say that. You can't ask me to say that." He shook his head as he sat there looking like his world had come crashing down on him. "What have you done to me, Lanna Davenport?" he muttered. "I was in complete control of my life, and then…"

I could barely see him through the tears that had filled my eyes. My anger had all but vanished, leaving me standing there with nothing but pain and confusion and heartache tearing through me. Any strength I thought I had was gone. And I knew crying wouldn't help anything, but I couldn't stop. I pressed my hand against my mouth to stifle my sobs and waited for my body to give out and send me crashing to the floor. This was impossible. Choosing between two men I was hopelessly in love with… I couldn't do it. Who could?

Suddenly a pair of arms wrapped around me, and Luke's hands rubbed my back so gently that I almost thought it wasn't him. But he smelled just like he should, and he felt so warm as I pressed my face into his neck and sobbed. "Hey," he whispered and touched his lips to my temple. "Hey, I'm sorry. I'm so sorry, Lanna. I shouldn't have… I'm sorry."

I clenched my hands into fists against his chest and wished things were different. If I had met either one of them a week earlier, I wouldn't be in this mess. I wouldn't be fighting a war against myself and having to reassure them that I cared and didn't want to see them hurt. I was finally at a point in my life where I could make a choice and pick my own path, and I felt like I was just standing there at the crossroads, frozen with fear.

"I know you don't really have a choice in all this," he said. "I get that, and I won't make things harder for you."

Except he was wrong. "I absolutely have a choice," I argued, no matter what my mother liked to think. She wasn't in charge of my life; *I* was. I just didn't know *what* to choose. Maybe it was a good thing all my choices were made for me because clearly I was no good at it on my own. "I just… I don't know what to do," I moaned. "I'm just making a mess of everything."

"Shh," he whispered, stroking my hair. "This isn't your fault, Lanna."

"Isn't it?" Pulling deeper into his embrace, I wanted to believe him. I was the one toying with their hearts. I was the one who couldn't make a decision between freedom and safety. "Luke, all of this is my fault."

"You're right," he replied, and my heart sank. But then he added, "If you weren't so damn appealing, neither of us would have fallen in love with you, and we could have avoided all of this." His voice had gotten lighter, a little closer to the usual teasing I got from him.

I couldn't help but focus on one little part of what he said: "You love me?" I'd never heard Luke say the words, and I desperately wanted him to.

The laugh that came out of him was deep in his chest, and I felt it ripple through me and give me some strength back. "What do you think?"

I needed to stop crying. I had to lighten the mood before I broke any more. And the only way I knew how to do that was to latch on to his joking and hope it worked. "I don't know," I said and took a deep breath. "I'm pretty sure you were trying to torture me all night with those little looks and accidental touches." I leaned my head back just a little, enough that my cheek brushed his.

His heartbeat skipped a little faster beneath my hands, and I was rather proud of myself for being able to have the same effect he had on me. "Pretty sure that hurt me worse than it hurt you," he replied. "And seeing the way Adam looks at you… God, I've never had a worse night."

This wasn't working how I thought, and things were getting too serious again. Pulling back even farther, I took his face in my hands and forced him to look at me. "I'm sorry," I said, hoping he could tell I meant it. Judging by the way he leaned closer, I figured he did. "I shouldn't have asked you to be there. But I…" I could almost taste him, and his nearness was painfully distracting. I was trying to apologize, and he made it nearly impossible. "I like knowing you're there," I finished. "Being able to see you."

"So I'm just eye candy," he surmised with a smile. "I see how it is."

He was so much more than that. He was the reason I was feeling brave, the reason I felt like I could make my own choices for my own life. He was adventure and excitement and the freedom to explore the world outside of my mother's perfect life for me. Pushing my hands into his hair, I pulled him in the last little bit and kissed him until my head spun. "You're everything," I whispered back.

I thought I had been ready to make a decision, but now that Luke was right in front of me, I felt more unsure than ever. And while I knew the choice would be harder than anything I'd ever known, I also knew in that moment that I had gone too far in either direction to turn back.

CHAPTER FOURTEEN

It took every ounce of strength to leave the stables and head back to the dark house, especially knowing Luke was still back where I'd left him. As much as I wanted to stay, I was exhausted. The day had been impossibly long, and if I wasn't careful I would end up doing something I couldn't undo. No, I needed to sleep, and I needed to give myself a chance to figure things out. Adam was probably coming over the next night, and I would likely run into Luke sometime during the day. Both of them deserved more than half promises and indecision, something I couldn't give them if I was this tired.

The cool night air was refreshing as I walked, and it seemed to clear my head of a buzzing I hadn't noticed was there until it was gone. My heart was slowly returning to a healthy pace, and my muscles relaxed more and more the closer I got to the house. Now that there weren't any distracting men around, I was finally calming down and starting to feel like I could think clearly again. Though I knew better, it seemed like I hadn't had that ability for days.

Halfway back to the house, my phone buzzed and made me jump a mile in the air. *So much for relaxed.* Because the text was as late as it was and completely unexpected, I pulled it from my pocket and curiously looked at the message. The second I saw it was from Adam, I felt warmth spread through me without even knowing what it said. Was it possible to miss someone who had been gone less than an hour?

You are everything, his text said.

My whole body seemed to go cold as I stood there on the gravel path leading from the stable. It was impossible not to realize I had said the exact same thing to Luke just a few minutes ago, only it didn't seem like the words meant the same coming from Adam as it did from me. My chest tight, I clutched my phone in my hand and tried to understand why I suddenly felt like I had lied to Luke when I said that. Didn't I believe my own words?

I'd meant them. I loved everything about Luke, from the way he was so optimistic to how he made me feel alive to the glimmer he got in his eyes when he smiled, a sparkle that said he knew exactly what happiness should feel like. Okay, yes, he was a little intense sometimes, but I cherished his ability to stretch my horizons and help me see that there was more to the world than the little part I'd seen of it. Even if he was a bit dramatic.

I love you, Lanna, Adam said in another text.

Adam wasn't dramatic. He was about as far from dramatic as they came, and I didn't have to wonder if he would criticize everything I did. Not that I thought Luke was critical—I'd call it constructive—but at least Adam didn't have me questioning myself. But I liked how Luke made me question things. He made me want to think for myself and search for the truth and make decisions. I wanted to be more when I was with Luke.

But I loved who I was when I was with Adam.

I loved *Adam*.

Back in that stable, I was almost convinced I loved Luke too. I believed that he loved me, just as much as I knew without a doubt that Adam did. But now that I was on my own, away from the pair of them and with no one to influence my thoughts, as they both so easily did, I felt a knot forming in my stomach. *I love Adam.* It was easy to think now, even if I hadn't managed to say it before.

And Luke? Luke had worked himself into a place deep in my heart where he would probably sit forever because I owed him everything. But did I love him?

I didn't think I did.

Not in the same way I loved Adam.

My chest ached with that thought because I had to tell him. He was still in the stables where I'd left him, and I had to tell him. Before I let myself overthink things, before the idea of him clouded how I felt about the real him. If I waited until tomorrow, I wasn't sure I would have the strength. I barely had the strength now, but I turned to walk back to the stables and do something I knew would break my heart.

And I walked right into the hard arms of someone much bigger and stronger than my gardener. They grabbed me before I'd even finished turning, wrapping around me in a vice-like hold that knocked the air out of me. My scream turned into a crumpled gasp. "Don't fight," a man hissed in my ear. His sour breath churned my stomach and chilled my limbs with fear. "It'll be easier if you don't fight."

"Who…" I choked. I didn't understand. What was happening? In my own backyard. He was going to… Oh God. *Help.*

"Munroe owes me money," he replied, and to my horror, he started dragging me toward the front driveway. I struggled, and he only held me tighter until I couldn't breathe. "I wanted the son, but I'll take his lover instead."

A ransom. The shooter! I fought for air and tried to scream again, but what little I managed he cut off with his hand. I clawed at him with my free arm but it made no difference. He was twice my size. He'd have me in a car before I could do enough damage to get free. Oh God. "Please," I begged and barely made a sound with the word. I tried to trip him, scratch him, whack my head into his, but nothing worked.

Suddenly I went flying to the ground, landing hard on my shoulder and rolling. My head hit the grass hard, and for a second everything seemed to go black. Through the pain, I fought to see what had happened. It was too dark. I heard grunting. Rustling. Bone hitting bone. Two people wrestled in the grass a few feet away, their silhouettes merely shadows in the darkness. I had to do something. Go for help, or—

A gunshot tore a shriek from my lungs, and one of the shadows collapsed. The other rose and came toward me, hands out. Terrified, I fought to crawl away but could barely move. He reached for me, and I screamed again.

"Lanna!" he said and grabbed my shoulder, sending a shock of pain through my arm. But it didn't matter.

"Luke," I gasped and struggled up into his hold in desperation.

"Are you okay?" he asked, and I could hear the fear in his words. He pulled me tight against his chest and held a hand to the back of my head as if afraid to let go.

Tears stung in my eyes as the last two minutes flashed across my mind again. It all happened too fast. I didn't understand. "Luke," I said again because it was the only thing that came to mind.

"We need to get you inside," he said, breathless, "before—"

The second gunshot was worse than the first. It echoed in my ears, through my ribcage, and for a moment I could only focus on the pain because it tore through me like a bolt of lightning to my chest. But if I had known then what came after, I would have ignored it entirely because it was inconsequential. Insignificant.

Luke fell first, collapsing to the side as he was ripped from my arms. I dropped to my knees a second later and fell beside him.

The last thing I saw were his eyes, so dark in the night.

So empty.

CHAPTER FIFTEEN

It all felt like a dream. Fancy dresses and flashing lights and tender touches and little explosions. Memories smashed together with reality. I saw faces I knew and faces I didn't and faces that shouldn't exist. Matthew. Ben. Kind smiles. Worried glances. Adam swam in and out of view, sometimes smiling but never in his eyes. I saw my parents. Shelly the chef. Even Mckenna Foster. But I never saw the one face I was most desperate to see. Not even when I closed my eyes tight and fought for it. All I saw were dead eyes.

Sometimes I felt a hand wrapped around mine. Sometimes I felt completely alone. Voices spoke hushed words, pleading questions, blunt statements. Someone even begged me to wake up. But I couldn't. I didn't want to. If I let myself think too hard, all of my dreams collided into one moment on a dark lawn, and I refused to let that be real. It was only a dream. Nothing more. Just a nightmare that would only be real if I opened my eyes.

"Lanna," a broken voice said. "Lanna, please. I can't... I need you, Lanna."

And I couldn't stay hidden anymore. My eyes opened when I didn't want them to, and the world settled on me heavy and thick. Everything about the room was gray. The walls, the couch, the computer monitor that said a bunch of things I couldn't understand. Even the sun coming through the large window was weak behind a gray layer of clouds. And then there was Adam. The only color in the cold and lifeless room, he held my hand tight and watched me through tear-blurred eyes, begging me to say something or do something or prove that I hadn't followed somewhere I shouldn't.

I knew I shouldn't make him suffer anymore than he already had. "Hey," I whispered.

All the air rushed from his lungs at once. "Thank God." He looked terrible, like he hadn't slept in days. Dark circles ringed his eyes, and his thick hair stuck out in a mess atop his head. He grasped my fingers so tightly that they were numb, as if he were holding on for his own life. If he let go even a little…

"Where's Luke?" I said.

Adam's grimace said more than his words. "Lanna…"

"Where is he?" I repeated, and tears swam through my vision. I needed to know. I needed to know that I hadn't spent the last who knew how long mourning for him if it wasn't real. Had it been hours? Days? It felt like a lifetime.

"Lanna, he's…"

"Dead," I finished, and the word tasted as awful as it sounded.

Adam's grimace doubled, and he dropped his head onto the bed. "They tried to save him," he said into the sheets. "But he was gone before…"

Before he hit the ground. "What happened?" I needed to understand.

Slowly lifting his head, Adam could hardly speak through his anguish. "It was Nathan Bartlett," he choked. "The client I told you about? Said Dad sold him a fake painting years ago, back when…when he first started. Dad refused to pay, and he's been threatening… Oh God, Lanna, if I had known he might…"

"What happened?" I repeated, shocked by how cold my words sounded.

Adam was alarmed too, and he stared at me for a moment as if he wasn't sure I'd really woken up. Swallowing, he searched the sterile hospital room for help but found none. "He came after you because of me," he said. "Hoped Dad would pay him to get you back. I don't… I don't know how Luke was there. Or what happened. Your dad heard gunshots and ran outside with a pistol, and he found you lying there next to…"

"Luke fought him off," I said and blinked hot tears down my cheeks. Everything about the night was too vivid, and I wished I could forget. "He got me free, and the other guy was shot. I don't…"

"Bartlett shot Luke in the back," Adam finished quietly. "The bullet went right through him and hit you in the shoulder."

I looked down at the thick bandage on my right side. Judging from where the bullet hit, it could have gone right through Luke's heart before it hit me.

"Lanna, I was so afraid I'd lost you. They said it didn't do a lot of damage, but you wouldn't wake up."

Didn't do a lot of damage. He couldn't have been more wrong. The bullet might not have hit my heart like it did Luke's, but that didn't mean it hadn't broken mine completely. Luke was protecting me. If I hadn't let Adam in, if I hadn't let myself feel something and show affection and try to prove to the world that I was better than I was, this wouldn't have happened.

The words fell on my ears like icy needles: "This is all my fault."

But it wasn't me who said them.

I turned my gaze back to Adam. He sat there looking ready to fall apart, his eyes red and his face pale and his whole body tense and rigid like I'd never seen before. "Lanna, if I hadn't..." He swallowed and tried again. "Deep down, I knew there was a chance. Dad spent hours holed up in his office in tense phone calls, and your dad kept warning us that things could get worse. Then there was that attempt on his life, and... I knew it was dangerous, and I still pulled you into my life. If I hadn't fallen... You were never supposed to be in the crosshairs, but he was there at your house to get to me, and he must have seen us when... I'm the reason he took you. All of this is my fault."

He was so overwhelmed by the guilt he felt. It only made my own pain worse, knowing he was going to beat himself up about this forever if I let him. I couldn't do that to him. Not to this poor, sweet man who had done nothing wrong. All the blame rested with me. "Adam," I said, waiting until he looked at me. "Luke and I..." I shut my eyes tight. I didn't even know what Luke and I were. Not anymore. But I had to keep going. "I met him out in the stables instead of going inside the house after the party. I shouldn't have..."

There was a lot I shouldn't have done. Every time I was reckless, every time I refused to make a choice, every time I pretended I was something I wasn't. Why couldn't I have just continued to live my life as it was and stopped complaining about how perfect it was? Maybe none of this would have happened, and I wouldn't have been standing in the yard in the middle of the night trying to sort through my ridiculous drama, and I wouldn't have needed rescuing because I wouldn't have bothered leaving the house.

I shouldn't have pretended I knew my heart when I didn't understand it at all.

"Oh, Lanna," Adam said.

I looked at him. His were not words of hatred or anger or even shock. They were pity. Compassion.

"Lanna, you can't blame yourself. Please, don't...don't do that to yourself." He tried to grab my hand, but I pulled it away.

"It's my fault he's gone," I insisted. Then I turned my head in the other direction and pretended to fall asleep because I didn't have the heart to listen to him try to convince me I was wrong.

* * *

Leaving the hospital was by far worse than staying in it. At least inside I didn't have a crowd of reporters and curious spectators swarming around me, even if I did have my older brother constantly watching me like he was afraid I was going to do something stupid. Apparently Adam had expressed some concerns about my wellbeing, and Matthew had immediately jumped in to see that I didn't fall into the same traps he had a year ago. He didn't have to fear much, since Luke was the reason he himself had stayed in the world. I would never make Luke the reason I left it.

But outside, the cameras flashed and the voices collided and I nearly broke apart and collapsed on the sidewalk beneath the chaos of it all. Only Matthew's arm around my waist kept me upright, and he hurried me through the crowd and glared at the journalists until we reached the car and he could safely stow me away, hidden from the world again.

"You'd think they had nothing better to talk about," Matthew growled as soon as the car started moving. "You okay, sis?"

I nodded and clenched my hand in a tight fist as I stared out the window. If my right arm wasn't stuck in a sling, I would have gripped the door handle. I hadn't been in a car since Luke had found a way to chase away the fear, but I no longer had his heartbeat to keep me calm. I wasn't sure if I'd ever feel safe in a car ever again.

"Adam said he'll stop by the house later, if you're up for it."

I nodded again, only because saying no would bring more questions. As much as I cared for Adam, seeing him only reminded me that the other half of my heart was gone. I'd thought I didn't love Luke. But if I didn't love him, why did it feel like there was a gaping hole in my chest where he used to be?

Matthew gripped my free hand between both of his and held it tight. He was quiet for a while, but I knew he had plenty he wanted to say. I couldn't tell if he was afraid to say it or if he knew I didn't want to hear it, but he let a full five minutes go before he couldn't hold it in any longer. "Dad said Bartlett won't be going free anytime soon. He won't get to you or Adam or anyone. Ever."

Did it make me a terrible person that I wished Bartlett had died too? He spent three hours on an operating table and got to live. Luke never had a chance.

"Dr. Chatwal said the damage to your shoulder shouldn't affect your painting, so that's good."

"I'm not going to paint," I replied.

Matthew's hands tightened around mine. "What do you mean? Why not?"

I shouldn't have said anything. My loving older brother wasn't going to just let a comment like that slide. "You know why," I replied and shut my eyes. I couldn't paint without wondering if Luke would come up behind me and tell me how to make it better. And he would never do that again. Every time I would pick up a paintbrush, it would only remind me he was gone. Because of me. I wasn't sure I could survive that.

"Lanna."

"Just let it go," I begged. "Please."

But he wouldn't listen to me. "Lanna, you have to paint."

"Why?" I argued. "So Adam doesn't lose face in front of his father after convincing him to sell something of mine?" The thought did fill me with guilt, but it was nothing compared to what I already felt.

"No," Matthew replied. "You have to paint because Luke wouldn't want you to stop. Do you know the moment he fell in love with you? Before he even really knew it?"

No, because he'd never gotten a chance to tell me. He had died thinking maybe I loved him back, and I had been about to tell him otherwise.

"He took you up into the hills," Matthew said, "and he watched you pour your heart out onto a canvas for hours. He'd never seen anyone so focused, so dedicated, so completely vulnerable and open, and he said he couldn't look away."

A tear slipped down my cheek, and I didn't bother to wipe it away. Another would inevitably follow. Maybe dying was better than listening to me saying something that would break his heart. But the moment I thought that, I felt sick. He would have been okay. Heartbroken was worlds better than dead, and he would have smiled through it.

I hoped he would have smiled through it.

I would never know.

"Lanna," Matthew continued, "he said he could have watched 'that girl and her brush' for the rest of his life and never gotten tired of the sight. You *have* to paint."

I finally turned to my brother and found tears to match my own. "I don't know if I can," I admitted.

"You have to," he said. "Please. For Luke."

For Luke. There was a lot I had to do for Luke, and I knew no matter what I did I would never be able to repay him for what he'd done for me. More than saving my life, he'd shown me how to *live*. No, I could never do anything to match what he'd done. To make up for what I'd been about to say to him. I did love Luke, but it wasn't in the way he would have wanted me to.

"I'll try," I whispered, and we were silent until the car pulled up outside the house.

I knew it was going to be hard coming back to the place he'd died, but when I stepped out of the car I could hardly breathe. His truck was still parked over near the shed, and I fought against sobs as I stared at it. If I didn't know the truth, he could be just on the other side of the house, laughing as he fought against a wayward sprinkler or planted a daffodil just for me. But I knew better, and I wasn't sure I was ever going to be able to set foot in the yard again. Every bit of it was tainted now.

"Come on, Lawn Mower," Matthew said, wincing even as he did it. He and I both knew he could never use the nickname again. Ben might have been the one who thought of it, but it would always remind us of Luke. Why, of all things, did he have to be a gardener? "Let's get you inside."

The whole house felt different, almost like it wasn't my home anymore. The last time I'd stood in this hallway, everything had been better. Not perfect, but better. Now I would have to wander the halls and try to ignore the shadows that tried so hard to look like a man in a catering uniform. What I wouldn't give to have that night back. I would gladly take the torture of Adam and Luke in the same room together over this.

"Dad's at the office," Matthew said slowly, "but he'll be home for dinner. And Mom…"

I turned toward the stairs. Mom was probably up in her room making sure she looked absolutely perfect before she made an entrance. She was the one I was least eager to see. "She didn't even come visit me, Matthew," I said. "Not once. Even Father came a couple times, and he was busy with Bartlett's trial. But did Mother even bother to see if her only daughter was alive? Of course not."

"Oh come on, Lanna," Matthew replied, surprisingly angry, and I stared at him. "Give Mom some credit. She didn't think you'd want her there, so she saved you the trouble of turning her away."

I looked back to the stairs, confused. "Why would I…?" I knew why. The last time we'd interacted, it hadn't gone well. That party felt like a lifetime ago, and I wasn't even sure if I was the same person I'd been.

"Just go talk to her," Matthew said.

I didn't want to talk to her. I didn't want an 'I told you so' or a lecture on getting involved with the help. I didn't want her to make me feel worse than I already did or start going off about how I was neglecting Adam and needed to put in more effort.

"Trust me," Matthew added and gave me a gentle nudge. "Go talk to her. I did."

I had a feeling I didn't have much of a choice.

I took the stairs slowly, doing everything I could to brace myself for that woman. What sort of person didn't even visit her daughter after something like I went through? I thought for sure she would have been there to spin a story for the reporters at least, but I doubted she'd even bothered to try. She probably had brunches to attend and neighbors to brag to and a future wedding to plan because she was so sure her schemes had worked.

But when I stepped into Mother's room, I found a woman I didn't recognize.

From as far back as I could remember, my mother had always been flawless. She spent a great deal of time and money to achieve it, but she was perfection itself and had made sure she shone as an example to her wayward daughter. But the woman who sat in her armchair by the window was an absolute mess. Frizzy hair and red eyes void of makeup and disheveled clothes I didn't even know she owned, she looked like she'd spent days on the streets, and I had no idea how to react.

The moment she saw me standing in the doorway, she immediately broke into sobs. "Lanna," she gasped and jumped up, rushing forward to pull me into a painful hug I didn't return, mostly because I was too shocked to move. A second later she leapt back in alarm and only briefly touched my shoulder in its sling. "Oh goodness, did I hurt you? I'm so…"

Sorry. The word she couldn't say was sorry. If she'd looked her usual self, I would have bitterly finished her sentence for her, but instead I let my anger dissolve away, leaving me simply numb. "You look terrible," I said.

She scoffed a little, but it was halfhearted. "I know I do," she said. "And you look…" She searched for the word and grabbed a tissue to mop at her nose. "Miserable," she settled on. "Oh Lanna, you look absolutely miserable. What have I done to you?"

And suddenly I was in tears, falling back into her arms in the sort of hug I couldn't remember ever sharing with my mother. It was awkward and unfamiliar, and neither of us were quite sure how to do it properly. But I didn't care. I needed my mom. She held me tight and stroked my hair and rubbed little circles on my back until I could breathe again, and the whole time she whispered over and over again how sad she was that I had to go through what I did. "If I had known," she said, and thankfully she didn't finish that sentence. We both knew what she would have done if she'd known about Luke.

"I loved him," I told her, even if I wasn't sure what that meant. "Mom, I loved him so much."

And still she held me and cried with me and said nothing other than soothing words. Eventually we moved to the bed and just lay there, quietly crying together. It probably wouldn't last, but for that moment I clung to the comfort I found there by her side. I fell asleep in her arms, and for the first time in years—maybe in my whole life—I could feel just how much my mother loved me.

* * *

There were less than a dozen people at the funeral a week later, most of them mechanics and landscapers. Matthew gave a short eulogy, but even he hadn't known Luke for very long. The few remarks made by his coworkers were vague but full of emotion. No one had much to say about the man who had somehow managed to be both an inspiration and a mystery to everyone he met. They just knew they would miss his smile and his positivity. The world was a darker place without him.

Adam was among the attendees, but he kept his distance. I knew he had planned and paid for the funeral and its expenses, but I couldn't bring myself to thank him. Not yet. But I was glad he was there, even if he stuck to the background. Knowing he hadn't abandoned me after everything was the only thing that kept me going. I wouldn't have blamed him if he left and set his sights elsewhere. Any normal man would have done that back at the hospital when I admitted there was more to my relationship with Luke than there should have been.

But Adam wasn't a normal man.

He came up to my side after they'd put Luke's casket in the ground. All the others had left, and Matthew had gone to wait by the car so I could have a moment alone. Surprisingly, I didn't mind having Adam stand there next to me as I clung to a dozen daffodils and tried to will myself to lay them on the new headstone. I needed someone else's strength, and Adam was quiet enough to lend it to me without interrupting my sorrow.

"I'm so sorry," I whispered to the stone. Luke's name was etched deep in the dark granite. It would live there for decades and beyond, the last remnant of a man whose life had been much too short. "You deserved so much more than this." After all the hardships Luke had gone through, *thrived* through, it didn't seem fair that a little piece of metal had ended it all so easily. I crouched down, gently resting the bright yellow flowers against the headstone.

There was so much I wanted to tell him, but I wasn't sure how long I'd be able to talk before I broke into tears again. "Seems all I do is cry lately," I admitted to the stone. "You'd probably laugh at me if you knew how often I do it, tell me I don't look nearly as pretty when I'm sobbing." And he would find a way to fix it. He was good at that, fixing my problems and making me feel better. Whole. Valuable. Like I was meant to be in this world because there was no one else who could play my part but me. I'd figured that part out over the last few days while talking to Matthew and Adam and my father and even my mother. We were all important in our own spheres. Vital. Just like Luke had been, since I knew beyond a doubt that there was no one who could replace him.

We all had a role to fill.

"You'll be proud of me," I continued quietly. "I figured out a way to help people like you. Like Josh the caterer. I'm going to start my own little business, helping freelancers get clients among the elite. Adam is helping me. He's..." I couldn't finish.

Adam crouched down at my side, his hand on my shoulder and his eyes on Luke's name. He'd visited me every day after I got home from the hospital, and he'd even told me stories about Luke, since he'd known him the longest. I had come up with the business idea soon after leaving the hospital, and planning this venture was a way to distract both of us from what had happened. I was pretty sure Adam needed it as much as I did. "I wish you could see her," he said softly to the headstone. "She's incredible."

I slipped my arm through his, gazing at him as he kept his eyes on the stone in front of us. "You deserve more too," I whispered, and the pain of my words hit me hard. I needed to let him go. Let him find someone who wouldn't make him wonder if she had only chosen him because her other option was dead.

Adam took a deep breath and slowly stood, bringing me with him. "If he was still alive," he said, reading my mind like he always did, "who would you have chosen?"

A freshly dug grave wasn't exactly the best place to have this conversation, but I could see the question eating away at him. He needed an answer, even if it was one that would only hurt him. I had thought I knew, but the grief I felt had made me wonder. "I don't know," I said truthfully. I missed Luke more than I thought I could miss anyone, and it was hard to know if things would be different if he were still here.

Would the choice really have been as easy as I'd thought out on the lawn that night?

Closing his eyes, Adam thought on that for a moment. How long before he left and never looked back? He'd stuck around so far, but there was only so much a man could take before he realized he needed to move on. And Adam seemed right on the edge of making that choice, pondering his decision long and hard and leaving me with bated breath as I waited. If he left, it would take me a long time before I could breathe again.

"So I had a chance," he said finally, and there was a tiny hint of a smile in his eyes as he looked at me again.

"You always had a chance," I replied. More than a chance.

"That's all I need," he said and bent down to kiss my forehead.

I didn't deserve him. "Adam, I can't ask you to—"

"I love you, Lanna. That hasn't changed. And I don't care how long it takes. Even if you never choose me, I'll be here for you. Simple as that."

Simple. I'd used that word to describe a life with Adam Munroe once, but it was far from the truth. There was no simplicity in the way he saw the world, nor in the pain that would follow me for a long time before I would ever be able to look at a daffodil or see the stars overhead without missing the one who gave that world life. There was no simplicity in the way I'd come to consider Adam my closest friend or how I really felt about him. About how much I wanted him in my life. There was no simplicity in the love I had for the man next to me.

"Stay close," I told him, meaning every word.

"Always," he replied.

CHAPTER SIXTEEN

It took me a year before I painted again. Not for lack of trying, but every time I'd pulled out my supplies, I'd sat in front of an empty easel for hours and never once put brush to canvas. At first I blamed the yard and the memories it held, but even after I moved to the Munroe mansion with my new husband, I still couldn't find the heart to do it despite the incredible views from the upper windows.

There was something about today that made me feel like I was finally strong enough to do it.

Adam found me in the kitchen early in the morning, where I sat in front of my half-eaten breakfast, and he didn't have to say anything for me to know he could tell something was different. His eyebrows low, he sat at the counter next to me and put his hand on my arm.

"It's been a year," I said.

"You have your paints out," he replied. They were sitting on the counter next to me, waiting for me to be brave.

I knew my plan would probably hurt him, but I felt like there was something fighting to get out of me. "I was thinking of going to the cemetery," I said and waited for his pain to show up on his face.

But he smiled, giving my arm a squeeze. "I think that's a great idea."

Tears filled my eyes. The last year hadn't been easy on either of us as we both worked through the guilt of what had happened last June, but I loved this man more than I ever thought I could love anyone. I had never once regretted choosing him to be in my life. "I love you," I whispered and leaned into the hug he offered.

"I love you too," he said. "So much. Do you need me to come with you?"

I shook my head. "I think I need to be alone for this one." Going to the cemetery had become a monthly practice. Sometimes Adam came with me, sometimes Matthew, but every once in a while, like today, I went on my own because I needed the chance to think through my own thoughts.

He nodded, kissed my forehead, and left the kitchen with his smile still intact, adding a soft, "Tell Luke hi for me," before he was gone. I didn't deserve him, and I hoped he knew how absolutely certain I was that he was the best man I could ever call my partner in life.

Too nervous to finish eating, I abandoned my breakfast and gathered up my supplies before I chickened out.

I ran into Matthew on the way to the garage, and though I was surprised to see him here so early, I smiled at the sight of him. "Hey," I said.

His eyes immediately slid to my bag. "You're painting," he replied, and his relief and happiness were clear in his voice. When he met my gaze, he looked near to tears. "How're you doing?" he asked. "I can't believe it's already been a year since…"

I was pretty sure I hadn't heard Matthew say Luke's name since the funeral, but I was glad to see my brother still looked relatively happy. Luke had been his best friend, and I was sure his death had hit Matthew just as hard as it had hit me. Not that he would ever admit to that. I loved my brother, but I had a feeling his smiles were as much to cover his own pain as they were to cheer the rest of us up.

It had probably been that way for most of his life.

"I'm feeling strong," I said, glad that it was the truth when Matthew relaxed a bit.

His smile warmed. "Good."

"How are you?"

He shrugged, his hands deep in his pockets, and leaned against the wall. "Life goes on," he said, which was more concerning than he probably realized. I didn't want him to just walk through life as a survivor; I wanted him to be happy. As happy as he deserved and more.

If there was any way I could help him like he had helped me, I wanted to do it.

"Mom was telling me yesterday about Catherine's latest escapade," I said warily.

My comment did as I hoped, and Matthew softened even more. "I think we might need to take our little cousin under our wing at some point," he said with a chuckle, and the idea of looking after someone seemed to do him good. That was who he was. He took care of people, and Adam and his dad generally played it safe with their art dealings, so Matthew hadn't had a lot to do as their bodyguard.

I was pretty sure he craved excitement, and our cousin Catherine would definitely give that to him if she ever came our way.

"I should go find Adam," he said, glancing at his watch. "Unless you need me to come with you."

Based on the dark circles under his eyes, I guessed Matthew had already been to the cemetery this morning despite how early it was. "I'll be fine," I said. "Thanks, Matthew." I watched him disappear around the corner, more grateful than ever that I had him back in my life.

When I reached the cemetery, the sun was warm and soft, bathing the place in a golden light that seemed to be sent from the heavens for me to paint. I took up my usual place near his headstone and set everything up, surprised how calm I felt. It had been exactly a year since the day we buried the man who saved my life, and I really had never felt stronger.

"I have you to thank for that," I said to the headstone, and tears blurred my vision again. I wished I had had the chance to tell him how much he changed my life. "I know," I said. "I'm being ridiculous again. You don't blame me for any of this."

As I started pulling out my paints, I couldn't help but think back on the day Luke had brought me out to the hills and taught me how to paint beyond what I saw. Until that moment, I hadn't really considered the idea that I wasn't limited to what was right in front of me. A canvas wasn't just a blank space to put some color but a means to capture my very soul and show the world who I really was. Without Luke, I might not have believed I was anything but what my mother made me.

I might not have even fallen in love with Adam Munroe because, without knowing myself yet, I wouldn't have known how easily I could *be* myself around him. Luke helped me see that possibility, and I had become something far more than what I ever imagined I could be.

"You should be proud of me," I said as I set up my easel. "I drove here. All by myself. And it was terrifying." I imagined Luke's proud yet teasing smile and couldn't help but match it. It had been a productive year in a lot of ways. "I have so many clients now I hardly know what to do with them all, and Mom has been throwing a lot more parties lately, probably out of pity. She keeps telling me I'll figure it out, though. Like she said, *nobody's perfect*."

A productive year indeed. Things weren't perfect between my mother and me, but they were getting better every day.

Everything ready for a paint session, I stretched my hands and looked out over the view. I'd never thought of cemeteries as pretty before, but after spending so much time there, I had come to see the beauty in them. There was so much I could paint, but I wasn't sure any of it would be right.

"I know," I said to Luke. "I have to paint something with my heart. Not my eyes. But I think I'm a little out of practice."

Gazing at his name etched in the stone, I started to form an idea. I wasn't sure I could even remember it properly, but if ever I were to paint something from my heart in that moment, it was the epitome of happiness. And while I could definitely say I was happy beyond my wildest imaginings, and my husband's contented smile almost always lit up his eyes and brought me warmth to my soul, I could think of nothing that quite compared to the smile I'd seen

early one summer morning in the back of a pickup truck.
All I had to do was close my eyes, and there he was.
A picture of simplicity.

The End

Special sneak peek of Book 2 in the Simple Love Series,

Growing Young

CHAPTER ONE

"Good afternoon, passengers. We will be landing in about ten minutes. Please return your seats to their upright positions and put up your tray tables while the flight attendants make their final checks. The weather in Sacramento is a lovely fifty degrees, and local time is 2:37 P.M.."

The voice overhead might as well have been condemning me to a month of agonizing torture. It was as if the pilot knew I was headed for my worst nightmare, and she wanted nothing more than to be absolutely cheerful and optimistic in light of my very real troubles. If I could just get up there and tell her exactly what I thought of her overly friendly voice, maybe she'd turn the plane around and head back to Maryland. I already had to get up ungodly early to make my flight and hadn't managed to ditch the driver Dad sent to make sure I actually got on the plane. It wasn't like sleeping on planes or trying to dodge chaperones was an easy feat, so I was exhausted.

"Is there anything I can get you before we land, Miss Davenport?"

I shoved my sleeping mask from my eyes to stare up at the flight attendant to had done his very best to make the entire flight miserable. I was sure he saw his friendliness as endearing, even helpful, but after he refused to bring me a good, stiff drink—"I'm sorry, Miss Davenport, but you're only seventeen. Would you like a soda?"—I decided he wasn't worth paying attention to. Yes, I was only seventeen, but that hadn't stopped a good many flight attendants from slipping me at the very least champagne. Most of the time it only took me a smile to get exactly what I wanted.

The awful man still stood there by my bed, all smiles and politeness that made me want to gag because none of it was real.

"Xanax?" I tried, though I could guess his response.

"Ginger ale?" he replied. His name tag said Hamir. I could only guess how he managed to sound so American.

With an exaggerated sigh, I shoved my many blankets off of me and struggled to sit up. "Don't you have some business class person to annoy?" I grumbled.

Somehow, his smile didn't even falter. Either he'd been doing this job for a long time, or that grin was permanently plastered to his face. "Your father was very specific in his instructions that you be well looked after, Miss Davenport." Which meant dear Hamir had been paid handsomely for the five-and-a-half-hour flight.

Oh, my father. Always trying to hide the fact he was not really a father at all. Luckily I turned out just fine despite his negligence, but he seemed to think I had no idea he was crap at the whole parenting thing simply because his money followed me wherever I went. Not that I complained about that part.

"Get this plane to go to the Bahamas," I told Hamir bitterly. "That's where I'm supposed to be at Christmas. Not stupid California." But no. Dad decided he and his new wife needed to go to Prague on their honeymoon and sent me off to whichever relative he could pay to babysit me. I should have been basking on warm, sunny beaches like I always did for Christmas, but while Dad got a vacation without me, I was left to scowl at the plainness of the Sacramento landscape as we descended.

I'd never been to Prague.

"That's unfortunately out of my power, Miss Davenport," Hamir replied, ever smiling and ever present. Better than I could say for my family. "I hear Lake Tahoe is beautiful at Christmas."

I had a good number of things I wanted to say to Hamir, but I held my tongue, only because I figured the woman sitting across the aisle from me would throw up yet again if she heard me. I had no desire to add my more colorful language capabilities to her motion sickness.

And though I gave him my best scowl, Hamir just smiled and indicated I should put on my seatbelt before he went off to check on the other first class passengers. So that was that. The one person who was supposed to take care of me had abandoned me to my old cousin and her husband who was probably a good twenty years older than her, as they tended to be. In my world, women went where the money was, no matter how old the man who had it.

Lanna Davenport. I hadn't seen my cousin Lanna since I was a kid, and Dad expected me to be happy about going to stay with her? She was ten years older than me, and the last time I'd seen her she was the most depressing person I'd ever met. She never wanted to play with dolls, and she never went shopping with us, and she was always knocking things over and tripping on her own feet. Dad said he wasn't sure how she could be a Davenport, that she had too much of her mom in her, and he always talked about her like she was going to be a disgrace to the family name. The whole family was a waste, he said. One son went and got himself killed in a car accident, and the other drank himself into embarrassment.

I was as shocked as he was when we got a wedding invitation in the mail a few months ago, telling us she was marrying into one of the more famous families in Northern California. How her mom had managed to pull that one off, neither of us knew. Her husband, Dad said, was a Munroe, which meant he ran one of the biggest art trade companies in the country. Part of me wanted to go to the wedding, just to see how ugly the man was if he settled for someone as pathetic as Lanna.

But even I had my standards.

And yet now I was stuck on a plane in the middle of December, about to spend about a month with the worst relatives, and there was nothing I could do about it unless I managed to avoid them after the plane landed. One more week, and I could have been left on my own. I was only a week away from legal adulthood, but Dad refused to accept my reasoning that I could survive a single week until that magical moment my age changed and I could do what I wanted. I suspected his new bride Daruska had something to do with that decision. Until he hitched himself to her Czechoslovakian wagon, he'd never had a problem with me taking a trip to Paris or Cabo on my own.

"Miss Davenport, welcome to Sacramento."

I shuddered as I followed Hamir off the plane. *Sacramento.* It couldn't have been Long Beach or even San Francisco? No, dear cousin Lanna had to think a place as lowbrow as Lake Tahoe was a fine place for a vacation. It was like she was raised in a stable. To think, I could have been in my favorite bikini by now, flirting with a cabana boy. But no, I was heading for the worst month of my life.

Unless I took matters into my own hands. As soon as I got my luggage, I had an entire airport at my fingertips, and if I played my cards right, I could be on a flight to Venice before anyone realized I hadn't shown up yet.

"Catherine?" a deep voice said before I'd even fully cleared the gate yet.

You've got to be kidding me. Dad must have really worked hard to make sure I didn't run off, and in a strange way it almost made me think he cared. But that was ridiculous. He didn't care about me arriving to my family safely; he cared about me embarrassing him while he was enjoying his actual vacation.

But when I looked up and locked eyes with the guy who had spoken my name, I found myself smiling just a bit. He was gorgeous, tall and solid and with a sharp jaw as his blue eyes took me in. "Catherine, right?" he repeated. "Lanna's waiting in the main terminal."

Had she sent a driver to fetch me? Probably. And I flashed him the smile that had gotten me a car for my sixteenth birthday from a man I didn't even know, because if this guy was going to be hanging around the next month, maybe it wouldn't be all that bad. "That's me," I said sweetly.

He held out a large hand for me to shake. "Adam," he said. "Shall we?" He headed for the baggage claim where my trolley would be waiting for me, and I slipped my arm through his before we made it very far. He gave me a look from the corner of his eye, and I smiled up at him, making his ears turn red. Goodness, he was tall. And smelled incredible, like Florida oranges. And though he put his hands in his pockets and hunched over a bit so he didn't stand out quite so much, the shyness didn't dissuade me from making a plan to charm him completely before we even hit the car. I could probably persuade him to drive me away from my fate if I had enough time to wear him down.

"Over here, Adam," a woman said, and instantly I prickled. I usually didn't mind a bit of competition, but I was too tired to fight for the affection of the handsome driver right now.

Adam perked up, standing straighter as a grin lit up his face. He slipped out of my hold and picked up his pace, heading straight for the pretty blonde who waved at him. Without so much as a word of greeting, he slipped his hands around her waist and kissed her like no one was watching, even though everyone in the area was.

Huffing, I grit my teeth and grumbled as I got buffeted by the crowd. It was the perfect time to try to make a run for it, but I couldn't help but glare at the woman who had already claimed my best chance at escape. She was about my same height, similar size as well, but she had the most incredible golden hair, long and wavy and perfect. I'd always wanted to be blonde, but I'd gotten stuck with boring brown. I'd tried to go blonde once, and it hadn't gone well. Mom had given me too olive a skin tone to pull it off.

"Catherine?" the woman asked, finally finished with her awful display of affection.

I stared at her, trying to figure out why she was looking at me with awe. I mean, I didn't blame her, and it wasn't like she was the only one in the vicinity who couldn't keep her eyes off me as I stood there. But there was something familiar about her, something in the way her nose crinkled when she smiled. It reminded me a bit of Dad.

"Lanna?" I gasped.

She broke into a grin, grabbing Adam's hand and moving closer. "Good glory, Catherine, you've grown up so much! I was half expecting you to still be in kindergarten."

How in the heck did awkward Lanna turn into Malibu Barbie? Well, Barbie in jeans and a t-shirt, but still. Put her in a dress and she would have fit right in with the parties I went to. But if this was Lanna… I turned to Adam and felt my face flush with heat as I realized who he had to be.

"You've already met my husband," Lanna said, catching my gaze.

Handsome hunk of meat was married to Lanna? I was suddenly glad I hadn't tried any harder to seduce him into taking me somewhere.

"And where did Matthew go?" she continued, unaware of how Adam seemed to hunch even smaller, which meant he'd probably noticed my attempts, even if they were small.

"Right here," someone new answered, his voice a little breathless. He came from the side, my luggage trolley in front of him and a ridiculous grin as he met my eye. "Jeez, Kitty, did you bring your whole closet with you?"

Matthew. I had a cousin named Matthew. Clearly he wasn't the one who died, but he didn't look like a hopeless drunk either. Especially when his eyes darted about, taking in the people around us in the keen way only someone who was trained to be alert and observant could. But he used my childhood nickname I hated so much, so he couldn't be anyone but Lanna's supposedly alcoholic brother. And I had a feeling he was going to make it much harder to get away from this place than I hoped.

"I think we've terrified her into silence," Lanna mock whispered to Adam.

"You do that to everyone," Matthew replied, leaning on the trolley and looking about ready to laugh as he took in whatever incredulous expression I had on my face. "So, Kitty, are you ready to see what West Coast Davenport life is like?"

Not a single one of them looked how they should. They were elites. High society. The best of the best. I should have recognized what they were just by the smell of their $1000 cologne and a wardrobe that screamed of wealth. But no. They just stood there in the middle of an airport looking completely…normal. Average. And I had a feeling their mediocrity didn't just exist in their fashion sense.

This was going to be the worst month of my life.

"What are we standing around for?" I grumbled. "Take me to my prison."

ABOUT THE AUTHOR

Dana LeCheminant has been telling stories since she was old enough to know what stories were. After spending most of her childhood reading everything she could get her hands on, she eventually realized she could write her own books too, and since then she always has plots brewing and characters clamoring to be next to have their stories told. A lover of all things outdoors, she finds inspiration while hiking the remote Utah backcountry and cruising down rivers. Until her endless imagination runs dry, she will always have another story to tell.